First Printing Lock 'n Load Publishing Paperback Edition 2019
Copyright © 2019 Lock 'n Load Publishing, LLC.
All Rights Reserved.
Printed in the United States of America in the State of Colorado
Lock 'n Load Publishing LLC
1027 North Market Plaza, Suite 107 - 146
Pueblo West, Colorado, 81007
Rev 7
ISBN: 9-781733-104142

DEDICATION

To Maya and Hiro

CONTENTS

INTRODUCTION

It's nice to be back here again. After writing about World War III in my other books, Lock 'n Load head honcho David Heath made me an offer I couldn't refuse and asked me to switch my focus to science fiction.

I didn't say yes too quickly. I had tried my hand at writing science fiction years ago and the results were mixed. After gathering years of experience as a writer and learning the ropes, I finally figured out what had gone wrong. My first clumsy stab at the genre was thwarted due to my own ignorance - I wasn't aware of SF's very specific story structure and the unique reader demands that made those stories work.

The prior existence of Space Infantry solved those problems - it came with a universe that had already been sketched out with broad but defining strokes. David had a specific vision of what kind of story he wanted to tell and the flavor it should offer. To top it off, he presented me with a manuscript that was a bit rough but needed just a little extra panache in places. To be honest, he was harder than he should have been on himself. David is a very good storyteller.

I used the existing storyline and David's advice as my handholds back into the science fiction genre. The result is what you have in front of you right now. If all went as well as we hoped, you'll encounter a group of characters similar to what you would find in the Space Infantry: Resurgence game from Lock 'n Load Publishing. Hopefully, this won't be the last time you've read about these people. There are plenty of fun stories to tell in this fertile setting.

Hard science fiction fans be warned: My aim with this book was to entertain. There is little here that might please hardcore aficionados.

This book is about action and it is meant to give readers a zoomed-in look at the men and women who populate the ranks of the Space Infantry team, much like those found in the game. Like Starship Troopers (the book and the movie - I love them both for very different reasons), my story is about how a group of people grow together in the face of battle. The wider political and military context is alluded to rather than spelled out, but I'd be happy to expand on this in future books if the demand is there for it.

Thanks always for purchasing and reading my books. If you're so inclined, drop me a line at the Lock 'n Load Publishing forums and let me know what you think. I'm notoriously bad at replying to messages, but I do read what's out there, and I take the constructive comments to heart.

Sincerely,
Brad Smith
April 2019

ACKNOWLEDGMENTS

As usual, I owe a big thanks to the folks at Lock 'n Load Publishing who had faith enough in my writing to choose me for this great project. David Heath 's suggestions and guidance were very helpful. Illustrations by Marc von Martial were on point, as always, and added much to the story. Thanks to Blackwell Hird and Gottardo Zancani for designing an excellent game.

SPACE INFANTRY
OUTPOST 13

BRAD SMITH
DAVID HEATH

VERTIGO

Will Hudson *pushed* through the wall of flames that engulfed half of Deck 34A. The immense heat radiated through his exoskeleton suit and seared his flesh.

Cradled in his arms was a limp figure, the last of the engineering team that had fought and nearly died trying to save the ship from going down. All Hudson had to do was get this guy on an escape pod then get ready to die.

Simple.

Three alarm blasts blared along the hallways - a final warning that few evacuation pods remained. Hudson's mask fogged up with each warm humid exhalation as he trudged forward. The entire ship shuddered right before another explosion ripped through its upper decks.

A sideways glance through the nearby window revealed a mass of debris flung off into space. Among the jagged pieces were telltale markings of the ship's control tower and forecastle along with its cargo of Athenium and other rare minerals.

The Kyushu groaned and creaked in the throes of death. It was clear now she couldn't be saved - not even with the herculean efforts of a thousand-man crew to douse the raging inferno that ran wild through it like a ravenous animal.

As one of the grunts aboard, Hudson's duty had been to help protect her.

When the minor refueling accident triggered a conflagration, he did his best to assist the engineering team. Hudson didn't know squat about all the fancy equipment – but he knew how to turn a wrench. Like the other 'geers, he had worked his butt off to save her until it was clear they had lost the battle.

Hudson planted his right foot and watched the suit's hydraulics respond in kind. The metallic boot bore down on the pod's hatch. A steel aperture swished open, and he set the wounded man inside the pod like a mother putting a sleeping child to bed.

As the pod doors rotated shut, the engineer's eyelids fluttered open. Hudson stood up and hammered on the release mechanism.

A placid feminine voice counted down from three to zero. The pod shot out of the hull. Its path toward the surface of the nearby planet was marked by a pencil-thin trail of light.

A deep rumbling welled up from within the bowels of the stricken ship. The approaching fires retreated as if they had been suddenly tamed by some higher power. Hudson understood the significance of this reprieve - the end had come and not a moment too soon.

The faces of his dead brothers and sisters flashed through his brain. A soothing thought calmed him, and he repeated it again and again like a mantra.

Soon.

A beam crashed down from the ceiling and sent Hudson tumbling along the long corridor. As the ship wrenched itself apart, his suit's alarms beeped and whined uselessly. He clung to a bulkhead and prayed that his death would be painless and quick. In the next life, he would meet them all again. Hudson could see the reunion now – a blissful celebration that would make him whole again.

The hull ripped open from stem to stern. Hudson was propelled out among the scattered debris of steel wreckage that was once the pride of the Colonial Government.

As he drifted toward the pearl-hued planet far below, Hudson closed his eyes and waited for the end.

It never came.

***

Nick Smith bolted upright in bed. The sheets were soaked in sweat and an icy barren sensation swept over him. It had been years since he had dreamed about the incident. Why had it returned now?

Although a few of the details were blurred by the passage of time, the nocturnal visions had recaptured the raw sensation of terror amid the flames and certainty of impending death.

The only thing missing was the aftermath - joining the Space Infantry, losing his old identity, and being assigned a brand-new name and face. Although it lacked death's finality, the SI program had offered a new life – and perhaps a way out of his rut of despair. In haste, he had signed the enlistment papers and resolved to never look back at what he had lost.

But now his old life was creeping back in. At first it had been little things – time spent gazing at old photographs or listening to old songs. Ever so slowly, it had ramped up into dreams and night-mares. Despite the second chance at life and the new people who surrounded him, a sense of solitude clung to his insides and refused to depart.

Afraid that doing so might open the floodgates even further, he had talked to no one about it. Instead, he had spent his nights chiding himself for thinking about his former life. How long had it been again since the accident transformed his life?

Three long years.

Will Hudson was dead. Long live Nicholas Smith.

The soft white glowing digits of the antique clock read 0429. A choking panic welled up. In less than a minute, the alarm would go off and something horrible would happen. Smith had no idea what it was. He just knew he had to prevent it.

His fingers fumbled over the machine's sleek upper surface. He pressed and flicked and turned at buttons and knobs and switches. But just like the echoes of the past, the "ALARM ON" light refused to disappear.

Soon, that bleating would fill his head and something worse than death would come and swallow him whole.

Like a grenade, he flung the clock toward the opposite wall with all the strength he could muster.

Halfway through its flight, the cord ripped out of the socket and cracked like a whip. When the machine struck the hard metal surface, it let out a sick garbled shriek before it shattered into a million pieces.

Wrapped in the silent darkness of the squad bay, Smith tried to banish the dread. His eyes closed and he conjured forth the soft warm sands of an alien beach beneath an endless blue sky. The sun's tender rays lingered over him while soothing waves lapped at the nearby shore.

It didn't take long for the sun to turn a bloody shade of red and for the sands to blow along a hot ceaseless wind. No matter how hard he fought it, the vision of paradise was robbed of him one sensation at a time. Very soon, all that remained was the dusty barren planet of his childhood.

As the fuzzy shapes gathered form in his mind, the door to the head clanged shut. With the gloom clinging to his insides, Smith rose on unsteady feet and padded over the cold metallic floor. Reaching for the door, the lights in the squad bay slammed on and Smith reflexively threw his hands up to shield his eyes.

Too late. The flickering florescent glare stabbed at his visual cortex like an ice pick.

"Dammit!" he shouted.

Over the sound of fast-running water came the voice of his roommate, Noah Stoltz.

"You can wait a freakin' minute."

There was little left to do but settle for a morning shave.

Smith grunted and turned to the mirror. Tepid water splashed over a face lined with regret at the previous night's booze-soaked celebration to the end of another grueling training day.

A lie.

It was more than that. Something deep inside him had shifted. Staring at the hard ridges of bony cheeks, the high forehead, and the angular chin was enough to propel the question to the front of his mind.

Who the hell am I?

The official answer for the last three years had seemed so easy. He was Nicholas Martin Smith.

It was a simple name that had been assigned upon joining the Space Infantry.

Since a small but notable percentage of his DNA could be traced far back to Anglo-Saxon descent, the possible list of names had been shortened to those that were most characteristic of such an ethnic background. A computer selected it as the best fit for his size, weight, and complexion – and that was all there was to it. He was untraceable – a non-entity among Union and its countless planets. Like all the others in the Space Infantry, he had become a ghost.

The cold steel razor scraped along a stubbled cheek. In his younger days, Smith had always felt more comfortable with a patch of facial hair to hide his face behind. It was as though a soft wall of hair could partially shield him from the unpleasant realities that one encountered throughout the course of a normal day.

Though that one simple comfort may have been afforded to Will Hudson, it was denied to Smith. Although he knew the reason for it was due to strict military regulations, it just seemed like yet another affront to his sense of self.

The idea flashed in front of his eyes for a moment, and again he tried to banish it. But this time, it wouldn't budge. Instead, it rang out loud and clear.

Quit.

He would leave the Space Infantry soon – disappear without a trace and spend the rest of his years back on Grimgate, where his family had lived, worked, and died. Maybe he could find a piece of his old self back there in the dirt.

The blade swept down again, revealing a smooth lean face that was not his own.

The shower door whooshed open and a tall athletic figure stepped out of the misty haze. Around his waist was wrapped a large towel, the last clean one in the squad bay. Smith considered strangling his squad mate with the pair of dog tags that clung to his neck but refrained. Sergeant White would have docked his pay for that.

"Lookin' good champ," said Stoltz, in his characteristic flippant tones. "You sleep in a dumpster last night?"

"Yeah," was all Smith could manage.

The word spilled out like a runny yoke. It carried no sense of the intended curtness that might have ended the conversation then and there. Stoltz failed to get the message and pressed on without due heed.

"You think it's possible we'll get through today without being zero-tasked? Because that would be awesome."

Smith lifted his wrist and checked a watch that did not exist.

"Y'know, breakfast is almost finished down at the mess," he said. "Better hurry. I hear the runny eggs and burnt toast are the best in the solar system."

Stoltz shrugged, threw some pit stick on, then ambled out of the head. At last, Smith was alone to nurse his self-loathing. He tried his best not to glance in the mirror as he finished shaving. The attempt cost him two tiny cuts astride his jugular. A trickle of bright crimson streamed over his fingers, and the smell sent his mind reeling back in time, twenty years in the past.

He kneeled over the body and wailed. The blood that pooled underneath it was still fresh and smelled of iron. Though young Will Hudson begged and pleaded his papa to wake up this instant, the man lay there in the dirt - shot down like a dog in the street by a jumpy sheriff during a miner's strike.

All they'd been asking for was a few extra credits a month. Thirteen of the men lay dead on the dusty ground, and none of them would see another penny. The voice of his older brother spoke the words that made it all too real.

Daddy's gone, Will. We're on our own.

When he finally came back to the present, he found himself standing in front of the mirror. His hands were stained with dried brownish blood and the water ran cold. How long had he been there this time?

He strolled into the squad bay to find Lisa Hayes sitting on his bed with the jagged shards of the alarm clock in her lap. Smith halted in his tracks as the diminutive girl looked up and locked eyes with him. A scowl tumbled across her thin face.

Her head swung slightly to one side, an effort to remove the unruly strands of blonde hair that hung in front of her eye.

Smith nearly smiled. She had no idea how beautiful she looked at just that moment.

"What is wrong with you?" she said. "Lemme guess. You can't shoot any bugs so you need to take out your aggression on a poor defenseless alarm clock."

"You planning to make a bomb out of that?"

Hayes tilted her head and gave a playful smile. "That doesn't sound like such a bad idea. You can test it out for me when I get it fixed."

"Hilarious. Care to tell me why you're here? Or maybe I don't need to ask." Smith took a step closer and grinned as he waved the hand towel in front of his waist like a bullfighter. Hayes appeared unimpressed.

"Those days are long over, buddy. Get a grip."

Smith knew the score but had no shame about their shared past. Years ago, they had been a thing. Once upon a time, she was an MP and he was a lowly recruit who went AWOL from training. It took her all of two hours to find his sorry butt flat broke and beaten up at the skeeziest biker bar in town.

She had gone easy on him in the official report – enough to help him avoid getting kicked out of the Space Infantry. Somehow, he had caught her eye despite all the bruises.

He looked her up again after graduation, and it was fun until things got complicated. Now they were in the same squad together and personal attachments like that had become a luxury that no one could afford.

"So why are you here then?" he asked. "And by the way, what time is it?"

"Stoltz said you looked rough," she said. "I wanted to talk to you about something important. It'll just take a minute."

Smith ran a hand over a dry scalp and tossed the hand towel in the corner. Hayes didn't flinch at the sight of his body.

"Look," he said. "If you think I'm gonna sit here and talk about my feelings like some kinda pansy, you know me even less than I thought you did. I'm hungover and I'm tired.

For most people, that's a cause for reflection. For me, it's a Tuesday. So let's cut the crap and get to the training room or White's gonna eat us for breakfast."

A wince flashed across her face before she collected herself. Smith knew he had just made a misstep, but he couldn't figure it out. He was fine! Why had she come here to dig?

"Suit yourself." She got up and sauntered to the door.

Smith worked his right leg into his fatigues while he chomped on a power bar.

"Suits me just fine," he muttered.

"By the way," said Hayes. "It's 0450. I've hidden your webbing somewhere in this room. You got ten minutes to get dressed and haul your cute little butt to the training room. Good luck!"

"What?!"

The door slid shut behind her. Smith scarfed down the remnants of his breakfast while jamming limbs into various holes in his garments. With his fatigues finally on, he searched high and low for his tactical web harness. It wasn't under the bed.

Not in the closet. Definitely not in the footlocker. It had been stashed, instead, under Stoltz's pillow. Smith cursed when he found it, then held the belt chest-high and pressed the buckle. The web gear harness shot out of the openings along the sides and slid around his waist and chest.

There was no time to check his attire in the mirror. Smith raced out of the room and counted down the seconds as he raced along the crowded corridors.

"I am dead! I am so dead! Five! Four! Three! Two! One!"

The door to the training room flew open.

Smith's gut churned.

In his head, an alarm was about to go off.

Something horrible was about to happen.

He just knew.

FOUR HUNDRED

Smith formed up with the nine other members of his squad. Sergeant Russell White, the tenth member, stood in the center of the enormous sterile training room with his hands on his hips and a sour smirk spread across his face.

Smith stared straight ahead and stood at attention, trying his best not to draw attention to himself. All he wanted to do was get through the morning without getting himself in deeper trouble.

So far, the sergeant had not acknowledged Smith's tardiness. Maybe for once, he would just let it go. There was always a chance, wasn't there?

"Corporal Smith! Nice of you to join us," he said. "Your squad mates were early this morning. Excellent work."

For Smith, hearing the word "corporal" in front of his name was still a surprise, even though he'd been promoted well over three months ago.

During his time in the army, he had only once gotten past the rank of private and was soon busted down after getting caught sneaking back into base after curfew. He had intended to come back on time, but apparently the dozen or so beers had other plans.

In the Space Infantry, however, promotions were permanent and could never be stripped away. The drawback, of course, was the additional responsibility that came along with it.

Though Sergeant White was in charge of the entire ten-man squad, he would often break them up into two four- or five-man teams with Smith leading one of them. It made them fast and flexible - a lethal group ready to come at the enemy from all directions.

White began a slow clap that made Smith cringe with each long sarcastic beat. When it ended, the sergeant's voice boomed at them.

"Unfortunately, you all forgot that you are a team. And when one of you is late, then you are all late!"

A chorus of groans rattled through the squad. Shane Heath, who stood beside Smith, shot a withering glance in his direction.

"Way to go, Smith."

Heath had a way of making Smith's last name sound like a swear word. It was a talent.

"I sure am pretty pleased you sorry excuses for an infantry squad graced my presence this morning," continued White. "Because now you can all count together to four hundred while you do push-ups. Now, get on your faces and OWN IT!"

The squad fell prone in unison. Every time Smith pressed his palms against the hard rubber flooring and yelled the push-up count, Heath would rub it in by turning his head and screaming each number in his direction.

The numbers climbed, and it wasn't long before a deep heavy ache seeped through Smith's muscles like molten ore. Grunts and curses spilled out from the men and women lined up beside him.

Well into the third set of one hundred push-ups, Jesse Babe's arms gave out like wet noodles and he collapsed as if he'd been shot. He spluttered and coughed, nearly sick from the exertion.

Smith wasn't surprised. Babe was one of the smaller guys and lacked the upper body strength to keep up with the punishment. He had been steadily leveling up in the gym for the last six months, but he wasn't quite there yet.

Smith rolled over and wrapped the kid's hands around his neck then swung back again to the push-up position. The rest of his set was performed with Babe resting on Smith's back. At fifty push-ups, the additional weight wouldn't have been too bad. It would have been hard at a hundred.

But as he neared the four zero zero goal, Smith had found the end of his endurance. His entire body burned with each excruciating movement.

Down. Up.

"Three hundred sixty-five!"

His arms shuddered.

Down. Up.

"Three hundred sixty-six!"

His knees quaked.

Sergeant White's face peered down at him from two inches away.

"Why don't you just give up, Smith?" he said quietly. "No shame in any of it. All you need to do is stop. Haven't you had enough already? Just two little words. 'I quit'. Just say 'em and I'll escort you down to the office and help fill out your discharge papers. Heck, I'll even wave goodbye to your shuttle from the station window."

Babe's weight bore down on Smith like a ten-ton boulder. The sweat dropped off his face in sheets. Stopping seemed like a wonderful idea. His entire physical being cried out for a respite. Why not get it over with?

A sting of pride jarred his brain, and he peeked over at Hayes as she grunted in agony and pumped her arms against the floor. No – this was not the time or place.

What would she think of him?

With a defiant snarl, Smith hollered back at Sergeant White.

"Three hundred…sixty…seven!"

White's head made the tiniest retreat. Smith saw the flinch for what it was. The small victory gave him all the energy he needed to press onward.

Each count got louder and more bombastic as the push-ups continued. The magic number approached, and Smith heard himself cackling as he screamed it out. The rest of the squad was galvanized by the show and joined in. Together they hollered and howled with laughter. Babe rolled off Smith's back and joined in.

When they reached their goal, the entire squad sang out.

"FOUR FREAKING HUNDRED!"

Smith smiled. They had won. Tomorrow might be different, but today they were unbeaten. He nearly begged White for more.

The sergeant ordered them to recover and together they shot up to a standing position. White stood there for a minute without saying a single word. If the man was pleased, he showed no sign of it.

The rest of the morning was rounded out with a 10K run around the circumference of the station. After a five-minute break, the squad broke up into teams of four.

"The following squad members will report for zero-gee sparring. Noah Stoltz, Shane Heath, Maddie Davis, Jesse Babe," White announced.

Smith cast his eyes to the ground, trying hard not to dwell on the grueling task in store for him. Would it be crunches until failure?

Perhaps they would be told to field strip and re-assemble the station's entire armory in total darkness again. That was an unusual brand of fun.

The absolute worst task, however, would be to sit and do nothing. No talking. No movement. No sleep. Breathing was discouraged.

White often assigned these "zero tasks" when he was particularly displeased with the squad for some reason. Although the prospect of sitting around and doing nothing sounded heavenly at first, it made each unlucky recipient feel useless and miserable.

If that was the point White was trying to make with the "zero tasks", he had done a perfect job of it. No one had joined the Space Infantry to sit around on their butts all day.

"Daniel Cox, Lisa Hayes, Nick Smith, and P. Rob. Suit up. You're in the combat sim," announced the sergeant.

Smith's relief was only outdone by sudden intrigue. He knew only that he was about to get very busy. Other than that, there was no way of predicting what was about to come next. And that was the point.

The combat simulations ranged in difficulty from slam dunk "run and gun" kill-fests to un-winnable firefights that wiped out the entire team in minutes.

The computer could even be programmed to realistically simulate any conflict that had occurred in the last five thousand years.

If the sergeant willed it, the team might find itself in the Wehrmacht battling the Russians amid the rubble of Stalingrad. Or they might be foot soldiers in Napoleon's army, fighting a last stand on the wind-swept fields of Waterloo.

Smith and his squad mates had experienced all of that and more through the power of the simulator. It didn't matter that the tactics and equipment were dated. The idea was to throw something completely unexpected at the group and see how they adapted to unique situations and overcame problems as a team.

Hayes stepped one pace forward to show she had a question. White nodded, giving her permission to speak.

"Sergeant, what's the sim sitrep?"

White wagged a finger at her.

"Come now, Hayes," he said. "Don't be a party pooper. That would ruin the surprise. By the way, an 'A' score gets all of you twenty-four hours of leave. Anything less than that gets the squad "zero tasked" for two whole days. Good luck."

The four members of the team gaped at each other with a mix of terror and despair.

"Well, there's one thing we can all be happy about," said Smith. "We get to die in the simulator before we die of boredom."

White tossed each of them a smartsuit and disappeared into the simulation command chamber. From there, he could decide every aspect of the simulated mission.

"Wonder what he's gonna throw at us this time?" grumbled Hayes.

Smith pulled the silver sleeve of the tunic over his arm. The smartsuit was an integral part of the simulation. It could tailor their appearance and gear to match whatever period and place they encountered. It also registered hits from enemy forces and took exact account of damage.

One time while playing the part of a Spartan during a simulated Battle of Thermopylae, the razor-sharp edge of a xiphos had sliced across Smith's lower leg. Though painful, the wound wasn't deep enough to kill him.

The smartsuit responded by constricting against his calf. Soon enough, the blood flow halted and the numbness set in. For the rest of the skirmish, he hobbled around as if he were really injured.

"I don't care where he sends us as long as it isn't Agincourt. All those arrows raining down on our heads," said Cox. "I still have nightmares about that!"

Smith stood up and checked that Rob's smartsuit was snug. The holy man's mouth twitched.

"What's up?" Smith asked.

"I should've told White to send someone else," he replied. "I'm not much of a fighter. I'll just slow you down."

Smith loosened the wire-thin strap that was wrapped too tight around the man's wrist. He slapped Rob's shoulder and grinned.

"Don't worry," he said. "You're one of the best medics this side of Sol. If we go down, you get to patch us up and send us out there again. We need you more than you need us."

Rob said nothing but Smith could tell the man was anything but reassured. The truth was he was partially right. Due to his own beliefs, Rob was a medic before he was infantry. He would fight when he needed to - but only when it couldn't be avoided. Though no one resented him for it, the reality was that it often meant one more squad member to protect and one less gun directed against the enemy.

As he stepped through the door to the simulator, Smith braced himself for whatever madness awaited him on the other side. The room flickered and dimmed.

His smartsuit bristled and wiry ripples of light coiled around him. The gear and boots he wore were his own – right down to the worn indents in the heel and the scuff marks on the toes.

A brief glance at his squad mates revealed all of them in their usual combat gear and weapons. A little wave of relief washed over him as he realized he was fighting one of his old actions.

The simulator's artificial intelligence spoke in a cheery feminine voice as the compound materialized around them.

"Sequence Initiated. Current Program set to Nostrum Incident."

"Oh man," said Cox. "Not again."

Smith shook his head as a twilight darkness descended all around them.

"I should have taken that discharge when I had the chance," he muttered.

JARDIN

Smith tasted the bile in his mouth as he watched the dark sky above ripple and render into finer detail. It was exactly as he remembered it. Standing on the virtual ramparts that ran the perimeter of the Nostrum Colony's compound, he surveyed the vast rocky distance.

Beyond the hundred-foot high walls lay piles of pulpified mutant bodies scattered for miles around. Dear god, what he would give to be anywhere other than here.

No one had fired a shot at the mutants - they had simply charged headlong into their own artillery barrage. It was a senseless waste of lives, but that was the whole point.

With this one viciously cruel act, the enemy commander had made it clear to the humans that they were vastly outnumbered - so much so that casualties mattered not one bit.

Smith knew what was next. The next wave would come soon - then another, and yet another - until the human's compound was overrun and every living thing within it was dead. It wasn't a question of "if" it would happen, but rather "when".

What did the mutants want with this dark desolate moon? It held no obvious strategic value and there were no major resources here except the very little bit of Athenium that had mostly been mined already by the human colonists who had lived and toiled here for fifteen hard years.

While the rest of the squad was embroiled in a bug hunt in the Outer Rim, Smith and the other remaining members were pulled off their well-deserved R&R to deal with an emergency evacuation here on this nameless moon.

Without any warning, the compound had come under mutant attack. Its inhabitants had sent out a distress signal, but the remoteness of the location had hindered rescue efforts. With only a handful of men, Smith was ordered to fend off the mutants while the population was herded off-planet one ship at a time in dribs and drabs.

The original mission had failed. After twenty-five harrowing minutes, the mutants had overwhelmed the compound's defenses and ripped apart most of its inhabitants. Smith and his team were only able to survive by making a run for it and calling for evac. In the grand history of the Space Infantry, the Nostrum Incident was not among their finest moments.

The fact that this was a simulation detracted not at all from the terrible feeling of being back here again and knowing what was about to happen. White had apparently spared nothing to faithfully recreate the look and feel of the compound. Even the pungent smell of the bodies stung his nose in the same hateful way.

None of it made much sense, but Smith had long ago learned that it didn't have to. The mutants had gotten bolder over the years and anyone who had access to the confidential reports understood that humanity had been drawn into an unofficial and undeclared state of war with them. Despite all that, neither the press nor the politicians made any mention of it. The civilian population - except for the victims of such attacks - was entirely unaware of it.

Regular military units were kept out of the action in favor of sending out the Space Infantry to deal with these incursions. What had started out as monthly assignments had turned into a deployment to the Perimeter systems for an indefinite period. It felt like applying a band-aid to an arterial bleed.

The Space Infantry were among the best the Union could offer, but there was only so much that small units could accomplish and being out on missions all the time was beginning to take its toll. Everyone in the squad was exhausted and on edge.

How long could they keep putting out these fires before someone stepped in and did something?

Smith spun to see the squad's infantry lander ascend from the docking pad in the middle of the compound. *The Mule* hovered for a moment, as if trying to find its balance. It then turned in a trembling arc until the engines spooled up into a blazing white glow that lit up the crowd-choked plaza.

Overloaded with civilians, the craft doddered like an old man toward the horizon then pitched vertical toward the starry heavens. Smith peered over the wall into the compound at the teeming masses that surrounded the docking pad. Twelve people had just been evacuated.

Only a thousand more to go.

Unfortunately, the evacuation was going to cost more time and resources than they could afford. The rescue fleet consisted almost entirely of a handful of orbiting civilian vessels that had responded to the colonist's distress call just hours ago. Further complicating matters were the docking facilities - or lack thereof. The compound had only one docking pad. It was not big enough to handle anything larger than a light freighter.

No doubt sensing the deep trouble they were in, the colonists surged toward the large flat docking platform while waiting for the next ship to arrive. Only the presence of a dozen constables kept the volatile crowd from unadulterated panic.

White's came voice over the comm set. "Alright, ladies and gentlemen. Here's the deal - I want you to THINK under fire - not just react. So I'll be tickling your brains the entire time with a quiz. Get a question right and I decrease the difficulty just slightly. Get a question wrong and I crank it up. Got it?"

"I've got a visual!" screamed Jardin. A sliver of grief tore through Smith's soul.

Jardin had died here - killed on this very mission. To see him again was like a punch to the gut. Though he knew this was a simulation and nothing would ever bring his friend back, a part of him wanted to try to save the guy.

At that moment, Smith hated Sgt. White for choosing to recreate this event. The tragedy was still fresh in everyone's mind, and surely the man knew he was dredging up wounds.

Jardin stabbed a finger out toward the northern horizon. Smith didn't need to look for himself - he knew already the enemy was charging again. It was just a feint. The real attack would arrive to the south, on the other side of the compound where Hayes, Cox, and Rob were positioned. A quick check on his helmet's uplink showed the vast stillness of the cliffs and mountains.

Cox's face popped up in the corner of Smith's display.

"Hey, we got nothing back here," he said. "You want one of us to help out at your location?"

"Negative," said Smith. "You know as well as I do, they're about to pounce on you over there."

"Yeah - but White might throw us a curveball and change things. Send the main assault your way."

Smith closed his eyes and tried to shut out the fact that he had been here before. It was true that White could modify any part of the simulation he desired with only the press of a button. He could play any mind game he wanted from the control room.

"You know what?" said Smith. "We try to outguess White or anticipate the simulation, we'll lose. If we fight the enemy the best we can - that makes it much easier. You get over here. Leave Rob and Hayes back there to cover the rear."

A chirp slid through Smith's helmet. Jardin froze in mid-stride as he scurried toward the corner parapets.

White's voice leaked through the helmet headset and he spoke as though he was addressing a class full of children.

"Alright, ladies and gentlemen. First question - What is the original name of Earth's first interstellar empire?"

"Too easy," said Hayes. "UPCG - United Planets Colonial Government."

"Ding! Ding!" said White. "We have a winner. When did the Office of Military Special Intelligence propose the formation of the Space Infantry?"

"2603," Rob said. After a nervous beat of silence, he threw in a cautionary "AD".

Jardin suddenly resumed his journey to the parapet. Smith couldn't help but react with a heartsick plea.

"Jarhead, I need you back here," said Smith. He heard his own voice cracking in the microphone and coughed twice in a vain effort to release the catch in his throat.

"Someone needs to cover that corner," replied Jardin.

The guy was right. The approaching mass of mutants would try to swarm around the defenders on the wall and probe the flanks to find the blind spots. Sure enough, they would find out that Jardin was the only one there and they would climb up over the growing mounds of their own dead.

Once over the top, they would swarm Jardin and pull him apart limb from limb. Smith still remembered the awful screams. What was left of the man was an unrecognizable heap of meat. No doctor could save him. Smith could only deliver the mercy blow.

God, how he hated White. This wasn't training anymore - it was sheer cruelty. Smith had half a mind to tell White to stop what he was doing - but it occurred to him that the sergeant probably would have taken such a reaction as a small victory. Instead of giving up, Smith decided he would do whatever it took to save Jardin and throw it all back into White's face.

"I'll take the corner," said Smith. "You take the wall."

With a sick feeling in his gut, he ran to the parapet and mounted the auto laser. After strapping himself into the seat, Smith hooked his fingers into the firing mechanism and pressed his thumbs down on the trigger. The massive weapon gave off a high-pitched whir as its six barrels spun up.

It was hard not to get too excited. Smith had to remind himself that firing the gun too fast would make it overheat. Once that happened, it would need precious time to cool down before it could operate again. Jardin had made that mistake and the results had proved fatal.

"Damn you, White," he said into his helmet.

The simulation paused again. White spoke up.

"I love you too, Corporal Smith," he said. "Next question might decide who lives and who dies. Are you ready? What was the original purpose of the Space Infantry?"

"That was before first contact," said Cox. "The government used the SI as a frontier police force. Mainly putting down rebellions in the Perimeter and dealing with secession attempts in the Outer and Deep Ranges. They were used on a much larger scale back then. Nothing like what we have today. Now we work in small groups. Light infantry teams. Mobile and deadly!"

The simulation world resumed with the angry howl of mutants rushing straight toward the walls from the north. The approaching army held no formation. It was just a teeming mindless horde of mottled flesh.

They bore no weapons - they had no use for them. Numbers alone were on their side. Ravenous and without fear, the mutants would never retreat a single step from their goal. Onward they would march until everything and everyone was wiped out in their path.

Smith spooled up the auto laser and fired a thick streak of white fire into the closest ranks.

His heart raced as he kept the trigger pressed down tight and watched the bodies drop. In mere seconds, the barrels gave off a soft red glow and a steady alarm pulsed from the weapon's control panel. The realization suddenly hit him like a hammer. The overheat buzzer held the exact same tone as the alarm clock in his room.

Smith licked his lips and squeezed his eyes shut as the sweat cascaded down his face and pooled at the bottom of his helmet's chin guard. A glance to the right revealed Jardin kneeling atop the wall, waiting for the hordes to come in range of their weapons.

The barrels of Athenium offered decent cover against any small arms fire that came their way. Although the mutants hadn't used any ranged attack weapons in the real assault, Smith wouldn't have put it past White to include one or two just to keep them on their toes.

Worried about the condition of the southern team, Smith checked in with Hayes.

"We've got a big group coming our way," he said. "What's new over there?"

Before she could answer, there came a loud slap and a deafening roar from the other side of the compound.

"The FREAK was that?" boomed Smith.

The sound of laser fire cracked off from somewhere near her position. Hayes's face popped up into White's viewscreen. Her eyes were as wide as dinner plates.

"You aren't gonna believe this, Smitty," she said. "We got Cybers over here. They've got RPGs!"

The mysterious group of robotic creatures were the newest in Earth's lengthening lineup of fearsome enemies. Five years ago, they had appeared out of nowhere, ravaging several of Earth's colonies for no obvious reason before disappearing.

No one had captured one alive - they self-destructed whenever they were damaged on the battlefield. The remains had been studied at length by UPCG scientists but all that could be determined was that they were a mixture of advanced technology and some form of alien life. The two sides were fused together so tightly that it was nearly impossible to tell where one half stopped and the other began.

Smith himself had only faced them once in his career. The results had been three squad mates dead and two wounded. They were deadly accurate with lasers and would take a tank's worth of punishment before they were destroyed.

"How many?" asked Smith.

Rob chimed in. "Too many!"

The gun's heat alarm ceased its infernal bleating. Smith fired another long stream into the tight mass of mutants. The decimation of their front ranks did not phase those behind them in the least. They simply marched straight over the crumpled bodies and limbs in a mindless parade of senseless death.

Jardin thumped out a string of grenades from his auto-launchers. The explosions tore into the oncoming crowd, sending bodies flying up in fiery fountains that lit up the darkness.

While Smith waited for the auto laser to cool down, he turned to see the next evacuation ship glide down from the night sky and pivot into a landing pattern five hundred meters above the compound. The crowd down in the plaza jostled forward and the handful of constables at the perimeter of the docking bay fired warning shots.

The simulation ceased and Sgt. White spoke up.

"So far, so good, troopers. Your answers have been correct. But things are going to get tougher from here on out."

Smith slammed a fist down on the arm of his seat. Who the hell did this guy think he was?

"Sergeant, we've been answering your questions correctly," said Smith. "I thought things were supposed to get easier when we did that. Not harder."

"Oh, you're talking about the Cybers?" said White.   "Yeah, I can see why you thought that. Actually, I did make it easier on you. I was originally going to make them Dark Faith."

Smith's breath cut off. He hadn't tangled with one of those before, but he had heard the rumors. They were the among the deadliest creatures in the galaxy. Fierce and fanatical and with a very high intelligence, they had fought two other Space Infantry teams and made short work of both.

Smith had watched the combat footage and caught a glimpse of one of the cultists in the short blurry vid. Its glowing eyes seemed to peer straight into Smith's very soul. Just thinking about them made him shudder.

Sergeant White let the silence speak for itself, then finally continued.

"Tell me as much as you can about Meridian 4. Impress me and I'll kill off a few of those cybers for you. Fail and I'll give you more."

A hostile quiet descended over the comms channel. Meridian 4 was a taboo topic for the Space Infantry. The whole debacle had reshaped the entire organization into its current form, but not without a whole lot of blood being shed. Smith gathered an angry retort in his mind. Just before he spouted off, Hayes pounced on his transmission.

"Meridian 4 was the location of the Blackroom base - that's where the SI Corps was located when terrorists struck in 2612. A suicide squad of insurgents infiltrated the base and guided a rogue asteroid toward it. After the strike, the entire planet was…not habitable.

"What remained of the Space Infantry were groups of independent operatives. Large-scale military operations were relegated to the Colonial Guards. The Space Infantry took on the role of small specialist teams based on Dark Stations throughout the galaxy."

Cox piped in, adding the coda to the story.

"Since then, the SI has remained a covert organization. All the members have had their deaths faked and provided with new identities. Many operatives are embedded with active duty crews in every system. Only a few people are aware we exist. Even fewer have any idea of who we are or what we do."

Smith bit his tongue until it bled. There wasn't much more to the story. Of course, there was the issue of recruits who didn't make it through the Space Infantry training or veterans who decided to opt out after seeing too much combat. Those guys were trotted off to MilSpecIntel - the intelligence-gathering arm of the UPCG.

When a trooper took that route, they were cut off from all contact with their former squad mates and recruits. Yet another new identity was created for them and that was that - all record of their accomplishments and deeds, no matter how selfless or heroic, was wiped out of existence forever. No ticker tape parades. No medals.

Smith couldn't stand the idea of being shuffled off into some desk job and put out to pasture. The fact was that retirement was a honey trap – you stayed put and enjoyed a soft end to your career, but for the rest of your life you would be monitored to make sure you didn't talk.

For most, it was a welcome reprieve from the perilous and often traumatic role as a member of the Space Infantry. To Smith, it seemed more like a prison. Jumping ship was the only way to real freedom.

The enraged bellows of the mutant army in the distance snapped his attention back to the present. He laid in a series of short rapid bursts of autofire into the crowd that had now reached the perimeter of the outer wall. Each time he pressed the trigger, the gunfire cut through them like a scythe through wheat.

The second evacuation ship took off and the group of colonists in the plaza were growing even more restless. One of the civilians clung to the long skids of the corvette as it ascended from the platform.

As it began its turn, the man lost his grip and tumbled two hundred feet to the ground. There was no way anyone could have survived such a plunge.

"Good news," announced Hayes. "White nerfed the armor on the cybers. They're dropping like flies out here."

"Nice to hear," said Smith. "Care to pay us a visit? We could use some help."

"You want me to leave Rob and Cox here?"

Smith's thoughts drifted toward Jardin. He so desperately wanted to save the guy this time. Another squad member would help ensure it. Cox had a twin rocket launcher that could cleave through cybers like a blade through butter. With Rob's help, they should be able to hold on a little longer.

"Tell Cox and Rob to keep up the fire. I need you over here for a bit."

Hayes tsked. "Fine with me. Sounds like you guys are having more fun anyways."

The third ship came screaming down toward the compound. This time it was a luxury shuttle, and Smith couldn't help but wonder who was organizing the evacuation efforts.

From the looks of it, the ship couldn't haul more than ten people. Well, it wasn't really his problem now. He peered down at the mass of casualties stacked up against the wall. Lumbering dark shapes clambered up the piles of corpses, heedless of the grenades that exploded in their midst.

There was no need to aim - Smith just swept the gun left and right, sending the enemies to topple in droves. Through the firing slot, a grotesque head suddenly appeared. Its angry gnarled features were a patchwork of fleshy suggestions. The eyes were wide apart while the mouth was a thin strip of cracked leathery skin. A slick pus-like substance oozed out of gaping holes that riddled its forehead.

The loathsome creature locked eyes with Smith and hissed, revealing a mouth full of razor-sharp teeth and crimson gums. The smell of its raspy breath was like the stench of a hundred bloated corpses laying out in the desert all day.

Smith pressed hard on the triggers and a hundred rounds spat out. The creature's head exploded in a fine crimson mist. Soon enough, another head popped up. Then two. Three. Each of them was met with a blast of the autogun. The weapon was holding up well so far, but soon there would be too many and he needed to get out.

"I think I'm done here," he informed the team. "Hayes, get back south. Fun time's over."

A glance out the window to the right revealed his team mates hard at work. Hayes and Jardin pulled the pins from a crate of grenades and dumped it wholesale on the mutants below. The grenades blew like a string of giant firecrackers, sending heads and limbs soaring out from the blossoming balls of fire. With a hundred more casualties inflicted on the teeming mass of enemies, Hayes scrambled along the rampart toward the southern perimeter of the compound.

So far, everything was going well enough. That was until Smith heard the bone-chilling scream nearly short out the audio on his commlink.

Seconds later, Hayes spoke up. "Cox is down. Rob's dead!"

"Hang on," shouted Smith. "I'll be over there in a second!"

He slapped the release on the three-point buckle that kept him secure to the seat. The straps around his body refused to slacken. Smith leaned over and wriggled one arm out of the harness just as a mutant shoved his head through the window. Another one appeared above it.

A long tendril shot from out of its mouth and wrapped around his leg. Smith stopped wrestling with the release button and found the autogun's trigger as his body was yanked toward a group of mutants who bayed at him like a pack of wolves about to feast on their prey.

Smith knew intellectually that none of this was real, but his body reacted quite differently. Raging rivers of adrenaline surged through his veins while his brain reeled from the threat and told him to run - to just get away from here at all costs. He kept the trigger buttons down until his leg came free from the thick snaking tendrils.

Before he could take any relief in his liberation, two meaty arms wrapped around his upper body. Hulking figures loomed inches away as the lights inside the parapet flickered and finally went dark.

In the pitch blackness, the stink of breath swept against his head. Unable to move his arms and legs, he sighed as the energy drained out of him. A pair of jaws clamped down on his arms and legs and neck. His blood gushed out in red streams and something dug into his chest.

Just before his gruesome death, the world shifted and a loud buzzing bit into his ears. The lights flashed on with a thunderous clap and the figures all around him rezzed out one by one until he was alone in the parapet.

The walls transitioned from smooth stone to yellow wiry frames. Bit by bit, the simulation world came undone all around them until the dark horizon disappeared. In its place were the barren surroundings of the simulation room.

Smith shielded his eyes from the harsh fluorescence that splashed down all around them. He took one last glimpse at Jardin before the figure of his friend pixelized and broke apart.

White's voice boomed again.

Get yourselves some lunch and be back here in an hour sharp. Word from on high is that something big is brewing."

The team staggered out of the simulation chamber and padded along the gangplank. No one dared say a thing about what had just happened. The trauma was too fresh.

Smith spotted White swagger over to them and clenched his fist tight. After the rest of the team slipped out to the shower room, he walked up to the sergeant, who stood there impassively studying Smith's face.

"Sergeant. What in the hell was all that about?"

White showed no sign of surprise or anger at the choice of words. By rights, the utterance should have landed Smith in the brig or even drummed out of the Space Infantry. Instead, the NCO's hand shot out and gripped Smith's arm.

"Jardin's death wasn't your fault. You couldn't have saved him. Not without losing something else. You make the calls as best as you can. Then you live with it. Do you see now?"

Smith's world crumbled a little as he gathered his thoughts together. So that's what all this nonsense had been about. White had known about the guilt and the pain.

He was trying, in his own way, to show Smith something important - to help him move on from Jardin's death. He wasn't sure the sergeant was right about his assertion - the simulation was too different from what he had actually experienced. But it was food for thought.

"Look. Something big is coming down the line," said White. "I need you looking forward - not back."

Forward. Not back.

The curious choice of words dug into his guts. Did White know Smith's plans? He took a deep breath and steadied his nerves. There was no way.

"What if I'm not ready for that?" asked Smith.

"Then we're dead."

White turned and stomped out of the gym.

Instead of eating at the mess hall, Smith spent the duration of lunch wandering around the long drab corridors of Station Hale. The words of White swept over him again and again. The time to act seemed upon him. He needed to make the decision right now – stay or go?

Through the starboard windows, his gaze fell on the pair of ships docked to the large oval-shaped station. The bigger of the two was *Thor's Hammer*, a huge spike-shaped dropship that was used exclusively to transport the team to and from deep space. It was ugly and lacked any sort of comfort that a station might provide.

Cocooned in its belly was the planetary lander, affectionately dubbed *The Mule* for its stubborn propensity to break down and refuse to work at inopportune times. Smith and Rob were its primary operators, a role that both men considered more of a curse than a blessing.

Next to the dropship was the station commander's Class IV Renegade Shuttle called *Mantis*. It was sleek and curvy, with not one but two short cylindrical light drives that hung underneath it.

Unlike the dropship, the angles were more than functional – they formed a testament to the designer's eye for aesthetics as well as function.

Smith smirked as his eyes wandered over the ship and considered the possibilities. Three jumps and he would be back near Grimgate, ready to pick up where his old life had left off. They would look for him, of course, but he would alter his appearance and name again. There were plenty of people who could do it for him – lots of underground clinics in the system that would operate for a fee.

After a careful glance around the station's empty corridors, he tapped the keypad next to the airlock. When the aperture slid open, Smith took a step back. White had told them that the SI codes would override the station's security measures, but Smith didn't really believe it until now.

Freedom was just ten strides away. All he needed to do was go back to his bunk, grab his stash of credits and be off. A few minutes later, he was back in the same hallway, lugging a ruck full of his life savings. Just enough to start over.

"Hey!"

Smith nearly tripped. Hayes stood there, her arms folded across her chest. Afraid he might tip his hand, he stood there like a schoolboy waiting for a scolding.

"Going somewhere?" asked Hayes.

"Uh…I'm in a real hurry," said Smith. "Can it wait?"

Hayes' eyes fell to the rucksack he carried and flitted over to the open airlock door.

"I need to talk to you," she said.

Smith bristled at the thought. He knew what was coming. She had already put two and two together and now would come a lecture about how they needed to keep together as a family and how the Space Infantry was his new home. It was all baloney and Smith didn't need any of that. Time was running out and he needed to move fast if he wanted to make a clean getaway.

"There's nothing to talk about," he said. "I can't do this anymore, Hayes. Let me go."

Hayes' face twisted with raw emotion. Smith considered his immediate future. If he left now, she would tell White. He would be caught before the first jump. Could he subdue her long enough to get away? Sure.

But there was no way he could bring himself to do it. She had been more than a fling – she was a friend.

"I won't stop you," she said. It came out like a whisper. Her eyes grew wet. "Not this time."

"Goodbye," said Smith. He pivoted to the airlock and took a single lonely step.

An alarm knelled.

Three shrill blasts just like the one in his room. Smith froze and closed his eyes, the sterile interior of the station's brig flashing through his mind.

White's voice spilled out in loud demanding tones.

"Squad! Pack your gear and be ready at the dropship in no less than three minutes. This is a Priority One situation. Repeat. Priority One."

Hayes sprinted off down the corridor. Ahead of him, just a few short strides away, was his shuttle and the chance to go back again. Before he could take another step, White's words came back to him for the millionth time.

Forward. Not back.

Smith heaved a sigh and rolled his eyes before making an about turn and making a beeline for the station's armory. Three minutes later, he stood outside the airlock nearest the dropship.

THOR'S HAMMER

The squad descended deep into the belly of *Thor's Hammer*.

White led them all past the cavernous training areas and spacious bunks that housed the teams on the way to and from the mission. When they finally arrived at the briefing room, he ushered them inside and waited until the weapons and ammunition were restocked and tracking IDs were checked by a small robotic quartermaster - an extension of the ship's Artificial Intelligence named Gideon.

Smith couldn't help but wonder what all the fuss was about. Everything so far had been pretty standard. White cleared his throat and spoke up. His voice was low and his eyes clung to the hands folded in front of him.

"What I'm about to tell you is Omega Classification," he said. "If any of this goes out, it'll mean the end of our careers and freedom. We'll all die in prison."

Throughout the ship's hull, a deep echo pounded like a heavy stone tumbling onto a thick icy surface. These were Station Hale's docking clamps releasing their grip on *Thor's Hammer* as it pulled away.

The effect lent an onerous weight to White's words. Everyone sat in rapt attention, their gaze clinging to the man's pockmarked face and leaning in to catch every word.

"We're headed to Cassandra. It's located in the Archimedes System just inside the Outer Range. I can't tell you much else other than it's a sensitive location. MilSpecIntel lost contact with them a day ago. No one knows why."

Davis chuckled. "That's it? All this cloak and dagger secrecy for a check-in! C'mon, sarge. You gotta be kidding."

White shot her a sober look.

"I'm not finished," he said. "There's a data card. Full of information that's vital to the security of Earth and its colonies. If a hostile group gets a hold of it, they could bring everything crashing down on our heads. We go in there. We get it. That's it."

"Good thing they put all that on a single card!" sniped Heath.

Smith tried to prod things forward. "What does intel suspect happened out there?"

Gideon's feminine disembodied voice floated throughout the ship like a daydream.

Slip drive beacon deployed.

White glanced at the readout on his wrist. "Jump in five minutes. I'll need to sum this up."

The sergeant thrust his open palm through the air in front of him. A transparent screen unfolded itself in the wake of his hand and hung in mid-air.

"Gideon. Playback Outpost 13 Secure Log. Code Two Two Nine Alpha. Bring the time to Oh Three Thirty Local."

The screen lit up and a formless series of images blurred for a moment until a map of the known galaxy came into soft focus. The tight cluster of Core Worlds sat in the center, surrounded by the Outer and Deep Ranges.

Along the edges were twinkles of light that represented the Perimeter. Smith tried hard not to look for his home planet. The scene zoomed in on the Outer Ranges in which one tiny pearl-hued planet revolved around a fiery crimson sun.

"Here's the planet of Cassandra. As you can see, there's just one small island on the whole thing. The island itself is rung by mountains and high hills.

There's just one valley at the center and that's where Outpost 13 is located."

Everyone leaned forward to watch, just like they were in an old movie theater. Normally, each of them would simply see all this on their own personal devices, but it wasn't too hard to guess that security dictated how such information could be shared.

The whole thing was bizarre to Smith. They had conducted so many covert operations before - what exactly made this one so special? He had a sinking feeling that this was about more than the contents of a data drive.

"Questions?" asked White.

"What's the plan?" said Heath.

"I'm shuffling the teams around a bit on this one. Stoltz. Murray. Cox. You're with me. We take the East Wing. Smith. Heath. Hayes. Davis. West Wing. Babe covers the exterior. Rob stays back here on the dropship for support."

Smith looked over at his team and considered how they might perform. Heath was ready and dependable though complaining as usual. Hayes seemed shaky and withdrawn after their encounter in the corridor. He could hardly blame her.

Davis was a firecracker and on edge. If he didn't keep her focused, there was a real possibility she would do something rash. Babe filled the fifth slot as the team sniper. The kid was a very decent shot but he was still inexperienced and prone to overdoing things. As the team leader, Smith would have to put in energy to tame the young man.

"What do we know about this place?" asked Cox.

"I'm uploading the layout to the squad's database right now," said White. The screen flickered then revealed a diagram of the outpost surrounded by thick forests with trees that stretched hundreds of feet into the air.

As the view panned in toward the blast-door entrance and through the gray interior, Smith pictured how they would move inside - clearing each room with quick and methodical precision. When the scene fizzled out, he looked over at each man on his team to see their reaction. Their faces wore the same look of determination as this morning's push-up incident.

"That outpost is huge!" said Davis. "What's something like that doing out in the sticks?"

White shook his head. "Beyond our pay grade."

"Surprise surprise," said Heath. "Seems like we're being ordered to do this thing with one hand tied behind our backs."

White cleared his throat. "This isn't a forum for complaints. We've been handed a job to do and we'll do it."

"Great. Just great. Do we know the exact location of the card?" asked Davis.

"It's expected to be in the command center," said White. "If not, we stay there until we find it or can confirm it's been destroyed."

Gideon's one-minute warning blared out like a trumpet all over the station. Smith sighed and scuttered over to the wall in unison with the others.

The ship quaked and groaned as the ionic drive spun up. It had been a while since he had been on a mission that necessitated its use. Most of the time, the ship's powerful light engines were able to move it quickly enough to get wherever the squad was needed.

As his hands met the safety wall mounts and the ship shuddered, the sensation of being stretched in all directions toward infinity took hold. In an instant, everything and everyone around him blinked out of existence.

Amidst the sheer nothingness that awaited, Smith was robbed of even the comforting blackness of sleep.

LOVELY, DARK, AND DEEP

The Mule set down at the top of a cloud-covered plateau a few miles north of the outpost. Though there was a docking pad right near the building, White had decided it was too risky to set down in the middle of a potential ambush. If there were hostiles within the base, it would have been easy to kill every team member as soon as they stepped off the ramp.

The line of Space Infantry trudged down the rocky slope and slipped into an alien forest where strands of light slashed down through a heavy canopy. The limbs of each tree resembled smooth curving tendrils instead of jagged branches. Smith gripped his rifle tight and took furtive glances all around him. After thirty paces, White's team bounded ahead while Smith and his men provided overwatch.

The forest was not expansive - only a couple of acres in either direction. But it was dense enough to hide almost any living thing. With his mind full of the possibilities of sudden and gory death, Smith counted ten then flashed a hand up in the air.

Davis shot past him with her medkits fixed tightly to her back. Hayes hurried after her with the heavy flamer cradled in her arms. Smith glanced at the moss-covered ground and tried hard not to consider the result of firing such a weapon amid all this vegetation.

Heath came next, grumbling as he disentangled a foot from the roots and vines that cluttered the forest floor.

Babe jogged ahead soon after.

Smith brought up the rear and nodded as his team charged past White and the others. Each step felt like a small victory for survival. If experience had taught him anything, it was that the terror never really went away.

As he raced past his teammates again and reached the point position, he took deep heavy breaths that fogged up his visor. The suit responded immediately, countering the humid formations with a short blast of icy air. Less than a second later, the faceplate was clean and his perspective unobstructed.

High above, the branches rustled on a windless day. Through the forest canopy, Smith spied a small winged creature glide along the treetops. One of the limbs shot upward and wrapped itself around the shrieking bird.

The struggle did not last long.

Feathers floated down as the struggle continued toward its inevitable end. There was an ungodly crack of bones and the shrill cries ceased. The tendril of branches snatched the prize and reeled it in like a fishing line. A series of notches at the top of the trunk opened up like a giant maw. The bird was flung inside and the mouth slammed shut like a blast door.

Smith's visor showed an incoming message from Heath. He blinked twice in rapid succession and the text unfolded just below his line of sight.

DID YOU SEE THAT?

Two more unopened messages slid in underneath it - one each from Davis and Hayes.

Smith didn't need to read them. Instead, he mouthed a quick message to the team and twitched his cheek to send it out.

It read simply:

STAY CALM. MAINTAIN COMMS SILENCE.

Despite the order, Smith couldn't help but feel that the burgeoning panic was somewhat justified.

After all, they were in the middle of a dark forest populated entirely of carnivorous trees.

If the mission briefing could not have bothered to divulge such vital information to the unit, this did not bode well.

Smith silently cursed at this rotten situation. It seemed whoever had passed down the mission orders and dictated the availability of information considered them as little more than cannon fodder.

After a ten-count, the other team dashed further into the trees. Cox, who was bringing up the rear, went flying when his foot slammed against a stump.

He crash landed in a thicket that curled around his limbs. The big man screamed. Hayes jolted forward and Smith shot a hand out to stop her. His other hand drew a vibroblade and hacked away at the slithering stems that bled over Cox's arms and legs. Hayes broke away from her overwatch position.

"Stand back!" she shrieked.

Smith's eyes went wide as she sparked up the flamer.

"No!"

Smith thrusted the hilt of the vibroblade at her. Hayes took a step back and grabbed it, then knelt down and sliced at the growing mass of tentacles. It was no good. For each branch that was cut, two more slid up and around his body.

Smith fired a couple of shots down at the ground from where the tentacles welled up. One of them lashed around his rifle and pulled. Heath grabbed at the thick rope-like branch and tugged in the opposite direction.

The struggle ended when Smith let go of his weapon, which was flung dozens of meters into the undergrowth. The team's attention returned to Cox's losing battle. Even with several vibroblades hacking away in unison, they made only scant headway into the vegetation that covered his body.

"Aaargh! It's crushing me!" howled Cox.

His breaths were labored and heavy as he writhed on the ground.

One loose tendril traveled over his chest then slithered around his neck. A pained gurgle came out of Cox's throat as the tree branch tightened.

"Hang on!" screamed Smith.

A flash of heat stung his cheek. Hayes ran up with the flamer. Her face was expressionless as stone.

"Stand back. This is gonna suck," she yelled.

Smith, Stoltz, and Heath scrambled out of her way.

"What are you doing?!" they shouted.

Before the question was even fully out, the sheet of flame erupted from her weapon and arced into the undergrowth.

A deep rumble blew among the trees, and the leaves trembled as if they were swept up by a storm. The blanket of vegetation retreated from Cox, who shot up from off the ground while clutching at his throat.

Smith watched the flames on the ground race along the stems and vines until they reached the nearest trees and welled up in red and orange sheets. The forest quaked and roared.

Without prompting, the entire team raced through the thick foliage. When they arrived at the tree line, Smith and the others collapsed in an exhausted heap as White and his team gaped at the wool-gray smoke that swept up into the sky behind them.

"Gimme a status," demanded White.

"Crispy," groaned Cox. "But alive."

Davis grabbed for a medkit and pulled out a clutch of syringes. Each squad member received a dosage of her special sauce, which brought their breathing rate down and, incidentally, helped to mollify everyone too.

"How did you know that would work?" asked Cox.

Hayes shrugged. "I didn't. Sorry."

Cox glowered.

Davis tapped his visor. "Don't complain," she said playfully. "You were saying the other day you were getting tired of the Space Infantry."

"That doesn't mean I wanted to get burned to a crisp or eaten by a tree," he said.

"God, I am so sick of this!" said Heath. "Can't we just have a normal mission for once?"

White told them to knock it off and the unit returned to a semblance of order.

"Eyes on the prize, guys. Let's move out."

The outpost was straight ahead. All they had to do was cross over the cracked chalky ground that led to its high walls.

The squad's intended pattern of movement and timing appeared on Smith's display. Shared among the wireless link in their helmets, everyone could easily see the intended approach to the building.

Red icons indicated White's team and a series of dotted lines showed its route to the East Wing.

Smith's team, shown in blue, would follow its lines to the West Wing. If all went well, they would arrive at the building at the same time.

"Let's do this," said White.

The team dashed along the rugged land in pairs, bounding past one another on the way to the outpost. As they neared, Smith sensed that something inside was watching and waiting for them. His grip on the service pistol tightened as he charged forward.

DISCOVERY

Smith sprinted past the perimeter security sensors and jogged to the wall nearest the west exit of the outpost. When the team stacked up near the door, he twitched out a signal through the helmet. Heath breached first, kicking in the door with enough force that it nearly snapped off its hinges.

Moving inside, the team swept the beams of their lights back and forth across the pitch-black security point. Looking over the table and monitors along the length of the room, Smith was struck by how neat and precise everything appeared.

"No sign of a fight here," said Hayes.

Heath chimed in. "No sign of anything - whoever was here just got up and left suddenly."

Davis plucked a coffee cup from a nearby table and held it up to her visor.

"That's weird."

"Lemme guess," said Hayes. "Decaf."

Davis held the cup out to Smith, who took it by the bottom rim and nearly dropped it when his fingers were scalded.

"Ow!" he exclaimed. "You could have warned me!"

"Lemme guess. Still hot?" asked Heath.

Davis nodded. "Like someone left a few minutes ago."

White's voice came over the comms.

"Sitrep."

Smith wasn't sure what to say. The team had breached into the building, but everything looked neat and organized. While it was true that White could have tapped into their video feed on his own, standard protocol was for the team leaders to report to each other verbally - there was only so much that a two by two inch screen could reveal about a situation.

"No sign of enemy contact here," Smith reported. "But there's some indications that someone might either still be around or recently left. You?"

"Nothing," said White. "Split up into pairs and keep searching. Report anything suspicious, but don't stop anymore to play detective. We're time sensitive."

Smith wasn't crazy about the idea of separating. If enemies were around, the squad members would be easy pickings in pairs. When they emerged from the security office, they found themselves in a wide hallway with doors on either side. At the end of it were a set of huge double doors that led toward the command center.

"Heath and Hayes, take the left side. Davis, you're with me on the right. Watch your corners," said Smith.

"This is a bad idea," said Davis. "We're vulnerable in pairs."

"Orders are orders," spat Smith.

Smith and Davis kicked open the nearest door to find a small series of cubicles no larger than a sailor's bunk. The blankets of each bed were pulled tight around the edges and tucked neatly into the corners.

Each footlocker was secured with a keypad, but a vibroblade was more than enough to open them. The contents were nothing more than standard issue toiletries, all folded and laid out with military precision. The uniforms and jumpsuits that packed the narrow closets were pressed and ready for a parade.

For Smith, the most shocking thing about it all was the lack of any personal property. It was pretty standard for even the most domineering of sergeants to let a family photo or a small memento slide by the regulations. Smith kept a snapshot of his parents and siblings taped to the inside lid of his closet door. Here, there was nothing of the sort.

"This place gives me the serious creeps," said Davis.

Smith clicked into Heath's channel to get a first-person view of a storage room stacked to the top with crates and boxes. A grunt of disappointment came over the air.

"Nothing," said Heath. "We got sent out here for nothing."

Smith was starting to agree. Except for the coffee cup, there was nothing here of any interest. Whatever secrets the outpost possessed were too well-hidden - if they existed at all.

The rest of the search was methodical and uneventful. There were no signs of life, and certainly no data card. Smith was about to declare the search a bust when Stoltz buzzed in, speaking too fast and excited for anyone to catch much of anything. White stepped on the channel and told him to repeat himself, this time more slowly.

"Offices," Stoltz said in a breathy voice. "Cameras. Lots of cameras."

Stoltz switched the view to his own perspective inside the main office section. Several dozen monitors were lined up on a series of desks amid a sea of cubicles. The various screens displayed what security camera footage of the team entering the outpost from the east and west sides. As the outer security doors swung open, the scene flickered then looped back to the start.

"Someone saw us coming," said White.

A tremble traveled along the length of Smith's jawline as he understood the very real possibility that they had lumbered into a trap.

Stoltz continued. "We also found -."

Babe's voice shot out over the comms.

"Incoming hostiles! Wow, there's a ton of them. Coming straight at you guys from the southeast and northwest."

The next thing Smith heard was a buzz of white noise that dug into his ears like an icepick. The audio dampeners kicked in and his agony subsided. The trackers in his helmet were absurdly distorted.

Although the map of the outpost was still accessible, the icons that showed the location of each team member were gone.

With the cybernetic extension of his helmet jammed, the entire world narrowed to his immediate surroundings.

He took a moment to shove back against the onset of claustro-phobia and isolation before grabbing Davis by the arm. With the press of a button, his helmet's visor retracted upward and the musty smell of the outpost filled his nostrils.

"Go find Sergeant White! Tell him we're covering for him in the garage," he barked.

Davis swept her visor up to reveal a face white with rage.

"You need me!" she protested.

Smith grabbed her rifle then shoved her hard toward command center door. "Don't argue. Just go!"

Heath hurried out into the hall, followed closely by Hayes.

"You guys are with me," Smith informed them. "I think I know where we'll be able to see our new friends."

Hayes scoffed. "There's three of us!"

Smith marched toward the door at the end of the hall.

"I know. I already feel sorry for them!"

STANDOFF

Smith stood before the bulbous window of the vehicle maintenance garage and took in the view to the southwest. Lurching towards the outpost was a horde of men and vehicles.

At the head of the group was a huge sleek turreted grav tank that skimmed the knee-high grass. Behind it, jogged scattered clusters of foot soldiers who wore an assortment of fatigues and clothing that offered no hint of identity or purpose. Even the weapons they held hailed from a variety of arsenals with no consistent pattern evident among them.

"Any idea who we're dealing with?" asked Heath.

Smith shrugged and cocked his weapon.

"Dead meat."

Both men wrenched up the garage door while Hayes dropped her flamer and switched to her rifle.

"What's the plan here?" she asked. "Drop a few shots and retreat? We can't fight all these guys."

"The plan is delay. We need to buy time for White and the others to escape," said Smith.

He crouched behind the cover of a half-assembled engine and let loose a burst into the nearest group of enemies. The lead infantry formations halted and dropped prone into the grass.

Seconds later, a clumsy volley of return fire slashed through the distance.

Meter-long sparks flew off the engine block and chunks of debris crashed down off the building's façade. Smith ducked and waited for the fire to slacken before leaning over a sliver's length to catch sight of the nearest enemies.

Peering through his rifle's scope, he watched for patterns and tried to work out their tactics. Among each group, a two-man team gestured and shouted while the followers among them moved and fired accordingly. Smith smiled and lined one of the leaders up in his sights.

The rifle's rangefinder blinked 680 as the firing dot settled on the man's forehead. Smith expelled a breath out of his lungs until they were empty. The automatic targeting system made furtive adjustments that kept the dot aligned on target.

WHAM!

Smith's rifle jolted as it released a bolt of energy that flashed and sizzled. The leader's headless body slumped over into the grass and disappeared.

The effect was electric.

The enemy halted its advance again and sprayed a hail of shots toward the outpost. The volume of fire was enough to send Smith retreating back behind the cover of the engine, which was now coated with long dark scars.

Miraculously, the grav tank sat there inert and unmoving. Its turret, offset from the garage by almost ninety degrees, did not rotate or fire.

After a ten-minute exchange of gunfire, Smith's rifle vibrated. Fishing through this web gear, his heart skipped a beat as he realized he was down to his last thirty rounds.

Over the din of gunfire, he hollered out to Hayes and Heath. "Hey! Conserve your ammo. Single shots!"

As if awakening from slumber, the grav tank stalked forward from its position. Five hundred meters from the outpost, it stopped and the turret rotated to face them.

Smith shouted. "Get outta here or you're dead!"

When he was just three strides out of the low building, a sickening "whoosh" crammed the air behind him. A hammer blow swatted his back and he tumbled forward as the entire garage was turned into a pile of steaming rubble by the grav tank's main gun. The ground trembled before the peal of the blast subsided.

Heath and Hayes groaned as they stood up.

"We need to get out of here right now," said Heath.

Smith shrugged. "You go," he said. "I'll keep them here."

"You don't need to do this!" said Hayes.

Smith checked the mag in his rifle. "Link up with the rest of the team. Go now!"

Hayes wouldn't budge. "You don't get it!" she pleaded.

A silver stream of rifle fire spilled toward them as they reached the rear entrance to the outpost. Hayes cocked the flamer and stood to one side, signaling for both men to get behind her. Smith watched as the first group tumbled in through the hole. The flames shot out and engulfed four bodies. The smell of searing flesh choked the air. Heath gagged and knelt on the floor.

The tinkle of a grenade sent a shockwave of panic through the trio of Space Infantry. They rushed back as a cloud of thick iron-colored smoke billowed up from where it landed. Soon, the entire corridor was filled with choking smog.

Smith clamped the visor down over his face and switched to thermal mode. The darkened corridor lit up in shades of green. The next group of hostiles who plunged through the hole were promptly dispatched by Hayes' flamer and accurate single shots of rifle fire from Heath and Smith.

They pulled back along the long corridor in a tight group, waiting for the final assault to crash through. Instead, the grav tank's gun boomed once again.

The round burrowed a six-foot diameter hole in the west wing. From where he stood amid the crumpled bodies and flickering flames, Smith could clearly see the new breach.

With another way into the base, the chances of survival - scant to begin with - were now dismally low.

A pile of enemy bodies lay in the corridor. Though the thermals in his helmet had rendered the smoke ineffective, the enemy hadn't realized it or didn't care enough to bother stopping.

Instead, they poured hundreds of rounds blindly into the breach and then sent a handful of guys tumbling inside. With enough ammunition, Smith and his team could have held out for days. But now they were down to their last few rounds.

The rifles and the flamer were dry long ago, and now it was down to the team's pistols. Very soon, it would be vibroblades versus rifles and that, as they say, would be that.

Heath scuttled forward through the lanes of fire and tried once again to snag a fallen enemy's rifle from the ground. As he neared, a red bolt of sniper fire flashed inches from his head. With no options left, he slithered back along the floor and waited in a crouch for the next group to burst inside.

This time, the hostiles were swift enough to toss in a couple of grenades first. A shower of hot jagged fragments slapped against the rubble and sent the team ducking behind cover. Something skittered along Smith's thigh like a bug and then stopped. Glancing down, he noticed the metal shard embedded in the leg of his suit.

"I'm out!" screamed Hayes.

The little flame that usually danced on the end of her lance flickered and died, and along with it went any hopes of surviving this ordeal.

Well, it had been a nice run.

A pair of men bounded through the breach in the outer wall, both of them spraying wild bursts of fire that bit into the air all around Smith and Hayes.

Heath, who had taken a shot to the abdomen and lay prone on the ground, leveled his pistol with a shaky hand and put a single round in each man. Before they even crumpled to the ground, Heath dropped the weapon and muttered a single bitter word.

"Dry."

Smith flicked open the vibroblade and steadied himself as he stood and hobbled. He swiveled and yelled out. "Get out of here! This time I'm serious. There's no use all of us dying here."

Hayes hesitated.

"You don't have to do this, Smith! You never listen. You just -!"

He turned on her, brandishing the blade as if he were about to jam it into her heart. His spirit nearly broke as he let out a growl and spat out the only words that might save her.

"You heard me, Hayes. Go! Or I'll gut you myself."

Her eyes narrowed as she spoke. The words shot out like a slap to the face.

"You don't want to save us," she said. "You just want a way out."

Hayes' dirty face twisted in a heap of emotion, then she fled from the room together with Heath.

As he watched her go, Smith wondered if she was right.

***

Smith hung back in the dark crook of a corner inside the outpost. The room was still largely intact with its spacious desks and banks of computer monitors still in neat little ranks. The wall-to-wall carpet, however, was another matter.

Blood had pooled on the floor underneath a pair of bodies that lay near his feet. The scuffle had been short and nasty - both men tore around a corner without due heed.

Two quick jabs with the vibroblade near the kidneys were enough to incapacitate both enemies.

Smith grabbed their weapons, but they were useless since the triggers were mated to the owner's fingerprints. The one good thing about all this was that he finally had an idea of who he was fighting: everyone.

The bodies were from a multitude of races. They were dressed in different fatigues and hailed from various military forces from dozens of systems. The messy tactics and haphazard leadership he had witnessed earlier now made perfect sense.

These men and women were almost certainly mercenaries. On this barren planet that offered nothing at all of any value, the only explanation for their presences was the data card. That deduction led his thoughts down a much longer road of questioning - the most important of which was - who hired them?

Buying an army of mercs with a grav tank would require more than just a fortune – it would require resources, expertise, and serious connections. That alone narrowed the list of suspects to maybe a dozen people and a hundred organizations – still too many to start busting down doors. To get to the bottom of this, MilSpecIntel would need plenty of evidence and a good dose of luck.

He checked his watch. Heath and Hayes had been gone a little over five minutes. That should have been plenty of time for them to get away from here. If not, well - he had done his best.

The crash-bang of grenades exploding in the outer hallway was followed by the howls of angry men. Smith found a nook among the desks and waited. If he could remain undetected, there was at least a decent chance the mercenaries would pass him by. When the coast was clear, he could try for an escape.

Smith was going to show Hayes she was wrong – he would find the team again and do it right. All that nonsense about jumping ship was on the shelf – at least for now.

A flash of movement caught his eye. Before he could respond, the entire world turned a fuzzy shade of white while his ears rang like an old church bell on Christmas morning.

The world spun.

Smith rested his arms over his head and prayed that he would not be discovered. Those faint hopes were dashed when a fist slammed down hard on his head with enough force to send him sprawling to the ground. Two massive kicks to the groin and chest and an angry snarl came next.

"Got ya!" his attacker shouted.

A seven-foot figure loomed over Smith. Slowly, the beastly figure removed his helmet to reveal a scarred reptilian face. His moth-eaten fatigues, two sizes too small, hugged his broad torso.

Smith gathered just enough energy to chuckle.

"What's so damn funny?" his interlocuter spat.

Smith coughed as a hand wrapped tightly around his throat and squeezed.

Through raspy shallow breaths, Smith replied.

"You hit like a little girl, fatboy."

The laughter rippled out of him in a series of anguished little breaths. A fresh round of blows landed on his chest and face. When it was over, Smith was flung like a ragdoll against the nearest wall. The two-second flight duration gave him just enough time to wonder if his little joke was worth it.

He lay on the ground like a crumpled piece of paper. His nerves were little highways jammed full of pain signals that bombarded his brain. Something warm filled his mouth and Smith retched blood on the floor.

"Grunt! Stop playing and search his body for the card!" said a high-pitched voice.

The big reptile leaned down over Smith, who tried to keep his body as still as a statue. His finger twitched at the thought of the hidden vibroblade at the rear of his belt. When Grunt turned him over, Smith knew exactly what he would do. He would grab the knife and plunge it straight into his attacker's thick ropy neck.

Instead, Grunt stood up and spoke defiantly.

"I am tired of following your orders, Mallick. I am done playing with him. Have at it."

The reedy alien approached Smith and knelt down. The hot stinking breath from the two tiny nostrils swept against Smith's face.

Large oval eyes peered at him, as if they could see deep into Smith's soul.

"He doesn't have it," said Mallick. "The one we want is waiting in the storage room."

What did that mean? Heath and Hayes had searched it earlier and found nothing. Had they missed the presence of the data card? If he could turn the tables on these men and interrogate them, maybe this whole affair would start to make some sense. Smith drew out a plan in his mind.

He would wait for the opportunity to take out Grunt. Then he would nail Mallick to the floor and ask some hard questions.

"By the way," said Mallick. "He's thinking about killing you."

Smith tried to wipe out all trace of the hidden vibroblade from his mind. The thin man reached around Smith's waist and plucked the weapon from the belt. The blade was tossed over to Grunt, who examined it in his massive hands with a snort.

"You were going to try and kill me…with this?" he said. "A bloody insult!"

"Nah…," said Smith. "'You were conceived in a dumpster.' Now, that's an insult. Or in your case…biography."

"Make your jokes, human," said Grunt. "You'll be pleading for mercy soon enough!"

Mallick swept a hand in front of Smith, who sensed something burrowing toward the center of his brain. Instead of resisting it, Smith shut his eyes and let a hollow sensation blanket his consciousness. The world was reduced to a fuzzy zen-like feeling intermingled with pain.

"He knows where the others are," said Mallick. "But he's fighting it. I can't get it here. Let's move to the ship and we'll do it the hard way."

Both men scooped Smith up from the floor as if he weighed no more than a feather.

They carried him back along the long rubble-filled corridors of destruction until they reached the gaping hole that once marked the wall to the vehicle garage. Smith smiled through bleeding gums as he saw the piles of scattered bodies.

Each corpse was a testament to the ability of the team to mete out punishment. That he had survived this long at all was a blessing. Whatever they had in store for him at the ship, Smith would make it last as long as possible before breaking. Time was on his side.

As they passed a squad of mercenaries who stood snarling at him, Smith stared right back at them and did his best to smirk. One of the men raised his rifle and it took two others to press it down and convince him not to shoot.

Thirty seconds later, they were close to the edge of a wooded area with no one in sight. Something hot cut through the air near Smith's ear. Mallick clutched the giant hole in his chest and dropped to the ground like a rock. Grunt let go of Smith, who face-planted into the hard soil.

Three rifle shots bellowed in rapid succession. Grunt gave out a throaty gurgle and Smith rolled over in time to see the giant fold in half, his body armor covered in laser scorches.

THE FALL

Smith lay in the dirt and waited for his senses to return. A flash of movement from the direction of the woods was enough to make him wonder if he was about to be killed or rescued. When the filthy face of Maddie Davis appeared, a smile came to his lips.

"Dear god, you're a mess," she told him. "Sit tight while I get you back on your feet."

As she unpacked the medkit, Smith watched two mercenaries in the tall grassy field run toward them. The first laser shot cut into the figure in the lead. His chest sparked with the impact of the bolt. The second blast was a direct hit from a rocket that tore the remaining man apart.

"I guess Cox made it," said Smith.

Without switching her attention from the field medical scanner, she nodded.

"Yep. Your leg's fractured, by the way. And…so are two of your ribs. Looks like they had some fun with you, Smitty."

Davis detached the square red base on the bottom of the kit and placed it on Smith's calf. It expanded a little and automatically wrapped around the limb then adjusted itself while letting out a small whoosh of air. Smith didn't notice the needles go in, but he sure recognized the sudden rush of adrenaline.

The microbiotics went to work, repairing his broken femur with lightning-fast speed and efficiency.

His first three steps were made with a painful limp. On the fourth, he hobbled awkwardly like a small child learning to walk again.

By the tenth stride, his injuries were completely healed. The medkits were very good - not enough to bring back the dead or help the fatally injured - but they could heal fresh wounds in a pinch.

When Smith reached the brush, he wore a big smile on his face.

"Hey guys!" he said. "Great to see you! We ran into a bit of trouble back there. Oh, thanks for killing Mallick and Grunt, by the way."

The rest of the team observed him as if he were crazy. Smith gestured to the pair of corpses that lay face down in the dirt.

"Nice to know you're on a first name basis with these guys," said White.

Cox reloaded his launcher and Davis packed away the medkit. Though still in a light daze, in a daze, he made out the form of Stoltz crouched behind a nearby bush. Fifty yards to the left lay the prone figure of Jesse Babe with his sniper rifle pointed to the rear.

"How did - how did you guys get all the way out here?" asked Smith.

White gestured over to Stoltz. "There's a hatch in the floor of an office. Leads to a tunnel. When the assault began, we went down and followed it. Comes out nearby."

"You guys find Hayes and Heath?"

"Negative. We thought they were with you".

"I sent them to find you," said Smith. The wonderful warm feeling began to wear off, only to replaced by guilt for sending them off to be captured or killed. "We need to go back in there and get them."

White shook his head. "Can't do that. At least not right now."

"Why not?"

"Because look at us," said White. "Our ammo's almost completely gone. We have injuries – worse than yours. And we also need support. We need to find out the real story here. Then we come back down and grab Heath and Hayes."

"How can you be so sure they'll stay down here?" asked Smith.

Cox gestured toward a wall of dark smoke in the distance that curled up toward the heavens.

"That was their ship," said the big man. "And it's also the reason why we have no ammo left. Those guys aren't going anywhere right now."

Smith hated the idea of leaving two team members down here. Even if they were already dead, their bodies would need to be brought back home for a proper burial. It was just how the Space Infantry operated – no one left behind.

Twenty minutes ago, he was ready to die in a blaze of glory. Now, the heroic attempt seemed hollow at best, especially after Hayes called out his motives for what they really were – a selfish attempt to shirk the duties he had signed up for. The attempt at sacrifice had backfired. Instead of saving Heath and Hayes, his actions had condemned them. If only he had kept them together, they would all be free now.

"I'm guessing there's a thousand guys between here and the lander," said Smith. "How are we gonna get there without taking on a mercenary army?"

Davis pointed to the rocky formations to either side of the outpost.

"I dunno," she said. "Go around?"

"That'll take time. Some of those cliffs are sheer and nearly all of us are hurt," said White.

"Well, we have to contact the ship somehow," said Smith. "Once Rob know what's up, they can lay down some serious firepower from orbit."

"We're jammed real bad," said White. "No contact with the ship. I'm willing to bet he has no idea what's happening down here."

Davis chuckled. "And neither do we."

Smith pointed to the bodies. "The mercs were trying to get to the data card too. I'm guessing they tried to infiltrate the outpost with an advance team and were detected. I'm willing to bet they saw us coming and decided to move in.

Probably thought we already found the card. One of those idiots said something about the storage room – but I know we already searched it."

"Let's get back to the dropship," said White. "We can scan the security footage from up there and talk to General Andrews. I'm willing to bet he can shed some light on all this."

JOURNEY

Smith took point as they trudged toward the tall rocky outcroppings that rung the island. His leg started to hurt a little, a sure sign that the stimulants were wearing off.

Getting to the lander was no easy feat. It consisted of dashing along jagged spines of rock and scaling the sheer surface of stony walls that blocked their path. Each step forward had become a test of endurance and willpower in an effort to reach the lander without being detected.

Occasionally, they would catch a glimpse of the world far below. All around the outpost were hundreds of dots. Each speck was an enemy mercenary, and Smith felt a hammer's blow of anguish at the prospect of Hayes and Heath being trapped somewhere within that perimeter.

Babe kept glancing down at them through the scope of his rifle, grumbling from time to time that he could take out a dozen or more from up here before they even knew what was going on. White ignored his pleas and kept pushing the group forward. Everyone else was strangely silent as they ventured along the rugged slopes.

The first indication that something was wrong came when a deep menacing growl bounced along the walls of the mountains and hills.

It was faint and far away but gradually grew louder. White called a halt to find the source of the disturbance, which Babe was the first to identify as the customized four-wheeled ATVs that several of the mercenaries rode upon.

"Those bikes are nasty. Twin guns mounted in the front. Looked like a pair of fifteens."

"Everyone shut up," said White.

The wail bounced off the rock walls. No one could pinpoint exactly where the vehicles were located. Minutes passed and White shrugged.

"We can't wait here all day," he said. "Probably a patrol. Keep moving."

The next stretch of rock was a winding path that led up to a narrow platform with a long drop on either side of it. The only way forward was to climb up a high wall that gradually leaned into a slope which led up to the peak. After cresting it, the rest of the hike to the lander would be much easier.

Smith dearly anticipated the end of the march - his limbs ached from scaling dizzying heights. But mostly, his mind reeled from the thoughts that bubbled upward.

Each challenge brought him a little closer to a sense of who he was and what it meant to be here among these people. Although his family back home was long gone, he had found a new one.

Each time the squad recovered from a setback, they forged an identity and a brotherhood that couldn't be denied. He would do whatever it took to keep that. When he returned for Hayes, he would sit down with her and tell her how stupid he had been. Ask for forgiveness.

Halfway up the sheer rock wall, Babe caterwauled.

"They're coming this way!"

Smith jammed his fingers into a crevice and, against all his training, glanced down. The world beneath him spun - a blurry mixture of iron gray and emerald moss. Gunfire cracked and sizzled through the air. Something hard slapped at the rocks above.

Just as the vertigo ceased, two huge boulders tumbled straight past him on the way down and slammed into the flat narrow cropping upon which Babe crouched.

The impact sent him sprawling toward the edge, and it was only the Sergeant White's grip that prevented him from plummeting hundreds of meters to his certain death.

Cox, who was already at the top of the cliff, leaned over and pointed toward the south.

"ATVs! Four of 'em!"

"I see them!" shouted Davis. Like Smith, she was climbing the rocky face and positioned about fifty feet straight up from Smith. There seemed little either of them could do from up here.

Davis was close enough to use her grapple gun to get a secure handhold at the top. Smith had another dozen feet until he could stop depending on grip alone to keep him from falling.

The buzz of the engines grew louder and Smith finally managed to spot the first one. It was a four-wheeled monstrosity racing along a narrow bend in the path that led up towards the team. The pair of one-fives mounted near the steering column flashed and the whole rock face trembled in response to being struck.

Smith hugged the wall as dirt and rock showered down upon him. It occurred to him that it wouldn't take much more to trigger an avalanche. If that happened, there would be nowhere to run and little to do but accept his fate.

Another ATV appeared behind it, braking hard to avoid the rear of the lead vehicle. Moments later, the first bolt of return fire thundered down from Cox's auto-launcher. The lead vehicle exploded in a fountain of red and orange flame.

The rear ATV driver answered with a stream of laser shots. Several rounds banged hard against the cliff, and again the deep grumble was followed by a cascade of falling debris. Davis screamed as she lost her grip, then plummeted straight down. Smith's heart fell as he watched her body tumble past. His hand shot down for the grapple gun near his waist.

The target lock on his visor lined up the shot for him. With a squeeze of the trigger, a razor-thin wire snapped out of the barrel and whipped toward the falling figure of Maddie Davis.

Her fall was suddenly arrested as the grapple's wiring went taut. Fifty feet above the narrow ledge, she dangled like a puppet from Smith's straining arm.

Davis swung back and forth through the empty air.

Smith zoomed in to catch a glimpse of the hook's barbs sunk into her suit. He gritted his teeth at the thought of the sharp metal tips dug into her soft skin. There was no question it was hurting like hell - but it was a lot better than the alternative.

"I got you Maddie!" shouted Smith.

The line snapped and she plummeted the rest of the way down. Her body pancaked on the ledge and she did not move. Smith froze, hoping to see some sign of life. None came.

Babe and White recovered from the initial shock of gunfire and scrambled for cover as they traded shots with the driver. Startled by the turn of events, the ATV reversed back down the narrow path. About halfway to the bend, Babe's sniper rifle cut clean through the driver's head.

The vehicle creeped towards the edge of the narrow cliff. White charged toward it. Just as the rear wheels cleared the ledge, he yanked on the steering column to keep it from tumbling off the side of the mountain. Babe threw down his sniper rifle and mounted the seat. A quick gear change was enough to right the ATV and bring it back to solid ground.

Smith climbed down as they inspected it. Neither man had noticed what happened to Davis. As he approached her limp body, her head turned slowly toward Smith and she muttered in sorrowful tones.

"Dear god. I think I broke my back!"

Davis lay still on the ground while Cox pulled out another medkit and applied it to her back. She couldn't walk and all feeling below her waist was gone. To add to her woes, four evenly spaced holes had been drilled in the back of her armor, each of them left behind by the grappling hook.

Smith wasn't sure whether to apologize or expect some kind of gratitude for breaking her fall. Instead, he awkwardly lingered near the captured ATV and listened to White talk about how it worked and point out the customizations.

"Change of plans," announced the sergeant. "We're riding to the lander."

"All of us?" asked Babe. "I don't think we'll all fit."

White eyeballed Babe as if he were the class dunce and continued.

"Not all. Davis and me. In case you haven't noticed, she's hurt. The rest of you will have to take out anyone guarding the lander and then get it warmed up and ready for takeoff."

"You guys will ride in later like the cavalry?" asked Babe.

"That's right," said White. "Just be careful. There's still a ton of bad guys sitting out there near the outpost. Once they see *The Mule* power up, they'll know something's going down. If that grav tank gets a bead on it, the whole ship will go up in one or two shots. Don't waste any time. When I see the engines flare, I'll head straight for it and bring Davis aboard. You better be ready."

"Sergeant, that plan sounds nuts," said Smith. "Maybe just goofy enough to work."

"That's nice but I don't remember asking your opinion about it. Anyway, once you're over that crest, you'll need to act fast to get into the ship and get it started. Any longer than that and we're probably all dead."

LIBERATION

Davis rode side-saddle on the back of the ATV while White drove. Once they sped off back south along the hills, the four remaining team members scaled the cliff, determined to get to the lander and get off-planet to regroup.

Smith watched as Cox climbed up the wall in giant vertical strides. The man had been born on an Outer Range planet that was nothing but spiky wasteland. The whole trek up and down the cliffside seemed like a day at the park for him. Stoltz made it up with a few stumbles but no real issues.

Babe, on the other hand, was having trouble. He slipped and overreached while trying to jam his hand into the little crags that marked the ascent. It was only with encouragement and a few dollops of abuse from everyone that he was able to make it to the top.

Smith stood up and let his eyes wander along the long flowing slope. Immediately ahead of him, resting at the top of the next plateau sat the lander. More than half a kilometer away, the figures near the ship were just tiny dots. The visor zoom revealed the enemies were all armed and coated in a sheen of armor.

"You want me to take them out from here?" asked Babe. The kid was already crouched and sighting in his rifle. Cox placed a hand on the barrel and lowered it.

"Shoot now and you'd ruin the surprise. We'd have a half a klick to run before reaching the ship," he said. "We need to get closer."

Smith sighed. Cox was right. And as much as he would have loved to put that launcher to good use, the weapon's signature would draw immediate attention to their location up here.

"Okay, get rid of anything heavier than a pistol," said Smith. He dropped the rifle after ejecting the magazine, then tossed everything into the dirt. Babe ruefully did the same with his beloved sniper rifle.

Cox had no such attachments. He activated the tamper-destruct on his launcher and left it on the ground at his feet. Smith smirked, knowing that any scavengers who picked up the weapon would not even have time to regret the decision before it exploded in their face.

"Redistribute your ammo and grenades," said Smith.

He had a vague recollection of training on a sim in the role of a British commando during a raid in North Africa. White had run four of them through a simulated mission to sabotage German supply trains in the rear areas. Only two squad members had survived. Smith was not among them.

With a rough idea of the route to the lander, they set out belly-crawling through the knee-high grass. Each second was an exercise in remaining as quiet as possible. Smith cringed at each rustle of leaves or the snapping of a twig.

At the lip of the plateau's flat summit, Smith sprang up and fired three quick rounds into the head and chest of the first merc he saw. His target stumbled back and then dropped to the ground.

Cox rushed forward and wrapped his arms around one man then simply flung him down the long bumpy slope. Both Stoltz and Smith rushed toward the lander. Despite the security keypad and autolocks, the ramp was already down and the doors open.

Smith gestured toward it and made a signal with his hand.

As they neared the ramp, a laser bit into Cox's arm. The big man grunted and reached for a grenade. Stoltz shook his head, but Cox was already in motion. He whipped the device straight up into the ship, where it exploded with a loud crunch.

Smith charged up the ramp, and hoped there were no other threats inside. He didn't know if Cox and Stoltz were behind him, but it didn't really matter anymore.

The whole operation had come down to a series of desperate acts and this was just one more in a long line of them. At the top of the ramp, his gaze fell upon the dead mercenary who lay on the deck, gasping for breath and clutching his wounds.

The walls were splattered in blood. Fragments of steel had burrowed into the walls and ceiling of the ship - along with several panels of the cockpit.

After a quick check of the rest of the ship revealed it was clear of enemies, the team assembled inside the cockpit. Cox nodded at the damage his grenade had done but gave no sign of regret.

Smith knew the guy well enough not to push it. In Cox's mind, he had seen an obstacle and removed it. Simple as that.

This time it was Stoltz who pointed to the south and barked a warning.

"Look!"

The huge sleek grav tank drove over the cracked landscape toward them. Its turret flashed and the entire mountain groaned as the heavy laser chewed into the slope.

SPITEFUL RETURN

"You think she'll fly?" asked Stoltz. His fingers wandered over the damaged control circuits.

Smith shrugged. "Only one way to find out. Fire up the engines and let's get moving."

"How long do we wait for White and Davis?" asked Cox.

Smith considered how much they had lost already on this mission. With two team members already missing, there was no way he would return to the dropship after losing two more. This was it - do or die.

"We wait as long as it takes," he said. "Babe, you keep a lookout while I try and get this thing working. Cox, cover their approach with the lasguns. Stoltz…try not to break anything."

The engines whirred and died. Thick black smoke belched from the control panel and Smith cursed Cox and his stupid grenade toss for the thousandth time as the fire suppression system kicked in.

A soft blanket of flame retardant poured on the little flames that danced along the co-pilot's instruments. By the time it finally shut off, the cockpit was slick with foam and reeked of burnt electronics. In desperation, Smith started pressing buttons and shoving wires into slots.

"They're coming!" shouted Babe.

"Who?" asked Smith.

"White and Davis! Woo boy, he's really going for it. He just bowled right through a couple of guys with that ATV."

Smith pleaded with the ship as he tried again to jump start its stubborn engines. Booze. Gambling. Bad relationships. He promised the gods that he would quit every vice in the known universe if only the lander would pity him just enough.

"Uh oh," said Babe. "That's not good."

Smith hammered on each button as he spoke. "Lemme guess. The grav tank."

Babe didn't have to answer. The ship rocked from another nearby blast. Just outside the cockpit, a fountain of dirt and rock leapt upward and fell across the lander in clumps. Cox fired a stream of laser fire back at it, which merely sparked off the thick armor plating of the vehicle.

"To hell with this," said Smith. "We'll do a cold start."

"Are you crazy? What about the shields?!" moaned Babe.

"We're sitting ducks either way!" The ship's systems whined as he pulled each one of them offline and rerouted all available power to the engines.

A glance outside revealed the ATV thundering along the sloping terrain to the north of the outpost. Laser fire arced across its path and White weaved the vehicle back and forth while Davis clung to him like an infant to its mother.

"Look at him go!" said Babe.

"Why don't you get out there and help?"

That was all the encouragement the kid needed. He jogged into the back and retrieved a spare rifle from the weapons locker, then dashed off down the ramp. From behind the cover of a nearby boulder, he fired again and again.

Each shot thinned out the herd of mercenaries that filled the distance between the lander and the outpost. Smith took some relief in seeing the grav tank's gunner get distracted by White's crazy ATV antics. The big cannon couldn't keep up with a target so small and agile.

Instead, the weapon missed and the heavy laser cut a swath of death and destruction through its own friendly forces.

As Smith got to the end of the startup sequence, Cox showed up in the cockpit complaining that the ship's weapons were no longer firing.

"Wrong station, you train wreck!" said Smith. "Stay up here and help me start this stupid thing."

Cox got down on hands and knees and fiddled with the wiring. Two presses of a button brought the auxiliary power generators to life. The air turbine deployed from the top of the ship and spun wildly, creating just enough energy to light up the cracked control panel.

Smith's heart raced as the display revealed a slow but sure increase in engine power. At eighty percent, he fired the ion accelerators and crossed his fingers. The familiar hum of twin engines filled the ship's interior. Smith slapped Cox on the back and whooped.

"Get back there and fire the guns, you big ugly beast!"

Cox stalked off to the rear of the ship. As the lander's engines spooled up to full power, he watched the ATV barrel up the nearest slope. Thick bundles of hot laser fire slashed all around it. When White was mere yards from the lander, he got off the bike and gestured toward Babe. The kid helped drag Davis up the rear ramp.

The lander hopped off the ground. A searing beam flashed across the cockpit, its heat creating an air pocket that made the ship tremble. Smith worked the controls and tried to keep his mind off the dozens of laser blasts that knocked against the outer hull.

One of the lander's engines nearly quit as he jammed the throttle past the safety limits. Instead of piloting the ship straight up toward orbit, Smith dropped down along the valley opposite the outpost.

With the mountain range between the lander and the grav tank, he sped just above the shoreline and the pale choppy waters before nosing up into the sky. After only a handful of seconds, the pastel colors faded to dark and the stars became visible once again.

Soaring through the upper atmosphere and into orbit, the communications channel suddenly cleared up and Gideon's smooth rich voice pleaded to be heard.

"Gideon, this is *Mule*," said Smith. "We read you clear. Give us rendezvous coordinates. We're on the way."

Rob's voice cut in, speaking in notes of excitement and relief.

"Boy, am I glad to hear you! I thought you were dead," he said. "Welcome back. All of you!"

Something about the comment cut like a knife into Smith's heart. "Well," he said. "Not all of us."

LOOSE ENDS

All eyes were fixed upon the ghostly holographic form of General Warren Andrew that stood in the middle of the briefing room. Everyone in attendance craved just one thing – answers.

"Sorry to be so blunt, sir," said Sergeant White. "But would you mind helping us piece together just what the hell is going on?"

Smith was worried that if he began to nod in agreement, his head might fall off. Instead, he kept his gaze focused on the floor and tried hard not to think of Davis, who was still in sickbay and under the watchful eye of Rob. Despite the broken back, her prognosis looked good and it would only take a few days for her to get on her feet again.

By then, Smith hoped, this whole mess would be long behind them and they would be chuckling together in the mess hall back on Station Hale.

The thought warmed him a little, and he considered for a moment just how tough the last few missions had been for everyone. Maybe White was right – there were things to look forward to. Things beyond carrying out orders and doing push-up or dying in a sim. There were good times to be had in the Space Infantry – if only he could learn to appreciate them just a little more.

He took a second to consider that tired glazed expression on Hayes' face at the airlock and how she let him go. Maybe she felt the same way about all this stuff.

If he could just talk to her, maybe they could both figure out a way forward in all this mess. Sure, being a member of this crazy outfit wasn't perfect. But running out on everyone wouldn't help. He could see that now.

"We're not really sure at the moment," said Andrew. "What we do know is that we've had several other key installations raided in the last twenty-four hours. I can't go into details, but this appears more and more like an orchestrated attack."

"By who?" asked Smith.

The general's head turned as if he were in the same room as the rest of them.

"Obviously someone with very deep pockets. If these are mercenaries, as you have already asserted, then whoever has hired them would need the resources of a well-funded government organization."

"There wasn't a whole army down there," said White. "But it was still impressive."

"I'm not talking just about numbers," said the general. "The money and manpower required just to pinpoint these secret locations would have been extraordinary.

"They would have needed not only one - but several espionage organizations to hack our clandestine network nodes then work their way through layer after layer of encryption without detection. Not to mention, they would have needed transport and supply.

"The evidence points squarely to an enemy alliance working against humanity. This can only be construed as a covert act of war."

Smith let the words sink in for a moment. The pattern of attacks and their growing frequency in months seemed to fit the theory. Someone had been nudging against humanity's borderlands. If what the general was suggesting was true, then this was all pointing to something very big on the way.

"General, there's something bugging me about this whole operation," said White. "The station was staffed…what happened to them?"

Andrews cleared his throat. "We can only presume they're dead. If you do manage to find any of the survivors, you're to treat anything they say or do as suspect.

We can't rule out that one or several of them opened a back door for them. It's the only way that the hack into our systems was so extensive - someone had to have provided them with passwords and encryption keys."

Something twigged in Smith's mind.

"General, I wonder how extensive the hack might have been. Could it have worked its way into our fleet networks?"

The general bristled at the suggestion.

"I very much doubt that. Our intelligence-gathering apparatus is entirely separate from our military. Besides, most of those systems are limited to sharing guidance and tracking information - useless for these kinds of small-scale attacks. Even with a thousand light transports and grav tanks, there's not much a mercenary force can do against our fleet."

White's jaw dropped.

"Something tells me, sir…that this isn't just a simple espionage operation. This could be the start of something much bigger than that."

"I agree, sergeant," said Andrew. "If you can retrieve that card, we might be able to investigate this. Failing that, it will have to be destroyed."

"Sir, we searched the base thoroughly. There was no sign of it. It's either in the hands of the mercs by now or it's destroyed."

Andrews paused for a moment before answering.

"It's not destroyed, sergeant," he said. "We know it's down there."

"Sorry, general. I don't follow."

"The card has a mechanism that warns us when it's been removed from the planet. Since we've received no warning signal, we can only assume that the card is still down there."

"Couldn't the card have been hacked somehow?" asked White. "As you mentioned, these people are professionals."

"I doubt it. The self-destruct feature is hard-wired into the card itself and doesn't depend on network activation. Tampering with the card physically would initiate the destruct sequence and trigger a memory wipe."

Smith turned to White. "I guess the plan all along was to capture the card and decrypt it right there in the base."

"How would they have known we wouldn't just drop a nuke on them?" asked the sergeant.

The answer struck Smith like a hammer blow.

"Because they'd have us as their prisoners. Those mercs wanted us to come here and investigate. My bet is they were hoping we would find the card for them too. If they wanted us dead, they could have just ambushed us on the way to or from the outpost. Instead, they waited until we were inside. If they were hoping we'd cave, they got more than they bargained for."

General Andrew piped up. "That may be so, but they did get what they came for. They have two prisoners and soon they'll have the data card if they don't have it already."

"With your permission," said White, "I'd like to take my team back down there and retrieve our men and the data card."

Andrew sighed.

"We can't take the risk that they'll decrypt that card and transmit its contents to whoever is paying them. Time is against us. The Luzon is on its way here. I can give your team two hours. After that, I'll be ordering a nuclear bombardment of the entire planet. If you're still there when it happens, sergeant -."

"We'll take that chance, General Andrews," said White.

"Then if there's nothing else, you'd better get moving."

THE ENGINEER

The next ten minutes were a flurry of movement and cursing as the team packed up weapons, armor, and ammunition. There was no detailed plan to any of it. Smith zipped open a ruck and tossed handfuls of magazines and grenades inside. When he finished loading the other bags, he noticed he was alone in the docking bay.

"Gideon, where is everyone?" he asked.

The AI chirped in response to the question. In a soft soothing voice, it told him where each of the team members were on the dropship's twelve enormous decks. Davis was still in the infirmary while Rob was working on a problem with the ship's computer.

One of the engineers, a curmudgeonly man named RJ, was with him. Struck by the oddity of the situation, he went up to the engineering deck to find both men hunched over a console.

"Rob?!" said Smith. "You comin' down with us? We need to get moving soon."

"Hang on a sec," he said. "RJ's tuned into the merc frequencies below. They're broadcasting to each other with some flimsy encryption. Buncha morons."

A tangled cluster of voices buzzed over the room's speakers. A flutter of static and interference smothered most of the transmissions, but Smith was sure he heard the words "hostages" and "package" mentioned at least once.

White stepped into the room and narrowed his eyes while he listened.

"Think you could clean that up?" he asked.

RJ shook his head. "No. What I can do, though, is triangulate some of their positions."

"Can you send that information down to us? Upload it straight to our helmet links?" asked the sergeant.

"Of course. I'm not an idiot."

"What about the jamming?" asked Smith. "It was so bad down there we couldn't talk to the dropship. Could barely talk to each other."

RJ nodded along impatiently. "Yes! Yes! I know all about that. I've jimmied something up to help. Your transmissions will work on frequency hopping now. Harder to jam and nearly impossible to pinpoint. If you ladies keep your pieholes shut and don't chitter-chatter like a sewing circle, they won't find you."

"Can you locate Hayes and Heath?" asked Smith.

"I've boosted your wireless capabilities. If you can get close enough, your link should pick them up. Well, their helmets anyway. Maybe their heads are still inside them. Who knows?"

Smith left the room together with White and Rob. As they pounded along the long corridor, White shook his head.

"If RJ wasn't so useful to us, I woulda popped that guy a long time ago," he muttered.

Smith said nothing but felt the same. The guy was arrogant, rude, and openly hostile to anything with a heartbeat.

RJ had grown up on Earth, the most privileged of planets in the entire union. Although Smith had never been there, it was widely known that its people lived in splendor and abundance. Smith had once mentioned the food shortages and occasional bouts of starvation that afflicted his home planet of Grimgate.

The guy had refused to believe any of the first-hand accounts, and stubbornly insisted that it was all propaganda. It was maddening.

The only good thing about RJ was that he lived alone in the bowels of the ship. His misanthropic tendencies led to deliberate attempts to make himself as inaccessible as possible - which worked fine for all concerned. Despite all that, he grudgingly pitched in during emergencies and he was quite useful when he chose to do so.

"Do we have a plan?" asked Smith.

"That depends," said White, "on your definition of such. That grav tank will shoot the lander out of the sky if it tries to land us in there. We're going in dark this time - jumping from low orbit. Get suited up for high altitude low opening.

"RJ found something very interesting through the engineering archives. Seems like Andrews didn't give us the whole map. There's another hidden tunnel under the outpost. We go in that way then locate the Heath and Hayes. If there's time and opportunity, we snag the data card. Otherwise, we bug out and use the harnesses for fast pickup."

Smith halted.

"Wait. Andrews wants the data card. Hostages are secondary. Don't you have it backwards?" he asked.

White's jaw clenched. "Negative, Smith. I'm pretty sure that for once, I got it right."

MY GRUBBY HALO

Smith had a beautiful view of where he and the rest of the team were about to die. The gentle gray curvature of Cassandra drew closer through the cockpit window of the lander.

Much of the land mass was clouded over from the vapor of the surrounding oceans that boiled like a broth. The few scientists who took any interest in the planet had theorized that such an odd geo-thermal situation would render the place incapable of supporting life, but the scant trees that dotted the single island were very much alive, as the squad had found out the hard way.

Everyone in *The Mule's* passenger compartment glanced at each other with the same ashen complexion of fear and anticipation. All it would take to miss the drop point was few meters of miscalculation or a mere ten-second delay in the drop.

If that happened, they could all look forward to landing in the scalding waters that dominated the planet's surface. No one would be able to save the unlucky souls, who would writhe and scream in the heat of such depths.

Much of what determined success would be Rob's piloting skills and although he was very good at maneuvering the lander, the simple fact of the matter remained that no one was perfect and blunders happened all the time.

A warning klaxon screamed and the squad snapped the pieces of the HALO suits to their armor.

An independent oxygen supply was next - just enough to keep them from passing out on the long ride down. Lined up in pairs, each of them turned around and checked the other's equipment one last time.

The strobe in the passenger compartment slammed on and everything was bathed in a red glow. Gideon's placid voice counted down the seconds, and Smith tried hard to keep his breathing steady and his mind focused.

The lander skimmed along, skirting through low orbit and decelerating just long enough for the drop. When it was time, the buzzer sounded, and the red light changed to green.

The rear door slid down. Depressurization was instant and the entire group was sucked out into the emptiness of space. In complete silence, they descended toward the pearl surface three hundred thousand feet below.

A fiery glow formed around each team member, and the heat shields sloughed off layers like a snake shedding its skin. Smith took a moment to appreciate the hush just before they found the upper atmosphere and a vast current of wind carried him along.

The needle on his altimeter swung counterclockwise so fast that it was hard to make out his current altitude. Every few beats of his heart marked the loss of a thousand feet and the island swept up toward him, enormous and beckoning.

It was at that moment that Smith had a clear view of his future. No matter what happened, he would stick by these people who came here with him. They were his family, and the only ones who would ever understand what he had been through. Like it or not, he was Space Infantry for the duration.

The last of his jumpsuit sheared off, lost to the eddies of wind. The oxygen tank, now empty, dropped listlessly from his back and tumbled end over end to meet the waters below. When he was less than a thousand feet above the planet's surface, Smith yanked the ripcord and heard the chute go "whump!" as it opened.

He was jerked upward just before resuming a much slower descent. Amid the thick cloud cover and suddenly he was alone, wrapped in its warm cotton-like midst.

With his visibility reduced to an arm's length, the sensation of falling evaporated until he felt as though he were hovering.

Very soon, he was through the soupy fog and his heart rate slowed as the others appeared, each team member tucked under the canopy of a razor-thin chute. Five hundred feet below, the landscape was dotted with dark specks.

As the seconds ticked by, the specks transformed into recognizable shapes. One of them, much larger than the others, loomed in their midst. The ground neared quickly and the appearance of an angular form made his legs and arms tense up as he realized they were all about to land in the middle of a clearing with a grav tank.

The group below obviously had not seen them yet - there was no incoming fire and the dozen or so mercenaries below did not scatter.

Smith pulled out two stealth grenades from his pack and flung them to either side. Just before striking the ground, he angled his body to bring himself closer to the tank. His chute sensed the impact and released automatically.

A quick check revealed the stealth grenades had done their job - the storm of flechettes that sprang out of them had managed to burrow into several mercenaries, who now lay on the ground in unmoving heaps.

Smith heard the boots of his comrades stamp the dirt as they landed nearby. The silent kill fest was underway. Space Infantry blades plunged deep into mercenary necks while silenced pistols fired point-blank into enemy faces.

The only thing left to worry about was the grav tank. Smith took two huge steps and leapt up on the hull as the turret slowly rotated. He grabbed the commander's hatch and pulled to no avail. Whoever was inside had thought enough to combat lock the unit. The only thing left to do was go loud.

"Cox!" he shouted. "Little help here."

The big man, who had just finished crushing the life out of one of the smaller mercs, turned and let the limp body drop from his arms. Smith pointed down to the tank. The turret stopped progressing as it pointed toward White.

Smith hollered a warning just before the coax spat out a thousand rounds. Cox charged from the flank of the vehicle to its rear. Smith slapped an explosive charge on the turret's box-like targeting mechanism and hoped it would be enough to blind the gunner.

Cox pulled out his light anti-tank weapon and went to work. Smith realized to his horror that he was on top of a huge piece of machinery that was about to be blown sky-high. Although he would have appreciated a warning, Cox was the kind of guy who preferred to let actions speak for themselves.

At first, there was no sign at all that the tank had been killed. Smith lay in the dirt and watched as the vehicle smoldered in the middle of the clearing. When the bang and pop finally came after a few seconds, the turret shattered like glass just before a column of fire leapt up from the hull. Inky smoke drifted up from the tank and wandered toward the sky.

Smith raced over to White, who was on his back in the dirt. The sergeant's blood-streaked suit sported two neat holes punched in the chest-plate. He wrenched off the helmet, revealing White's ashen face. His eyes were half-open and a thick sputtering cough spilled from his mouth. It didn't take a genius to figure out that the sergeant's injuries were way beyond a medkit's capabilities.

"You need to leave me here," said White. "We've stirred it up. You gotta get Heath and Hayes. Just get 'em. Don't worry about the card."

"You sure?"

"Leave me some grenades. I'm good. Just go."

Smith leaned the sergeant up against the ruined tank and placed a proximity grenade in each hand.

"I'll be back for you," said Smith.

"Nah."

Incoming laser fire bit at the air around the team. Babe fired a few shots into the distance, which seemed to keep the bulk of the mercenary forces at bay. But soon enough they would be here and that would be it for everyone. Smith gazed down at White.

"Thanks for-"

"You figured it out, right? We're your home."

"I got it."

"Then go," said White.

THE WORLD BELOW

The team sprinted through the clearing towards the tree line. When they got there, Cox paused for a moment before Smith kicked him in the backside. As they ran among the trees, incoming fire sheared off branches and sliced into the thick wooden bark. Splinters shot out everywhere. Two explosions sounded in the distance, and Smith knew that was the end for Sergeant White.

Ten seconds later, the remnants of the team arrived near the coordinates of the second tunnel hatch. Cox and Babe got on their hands and knees and dug through the leaves in an effort to locate it.

"Hurry up!" shouted Smith. "Those mercs will be here any second!"

"Where in the Sam Hill is it?" asked Stoltz.

Smith let his eyes wander around the little clearing as the cries grew louder behind them. It was with great relief he noticed that these trees were not the same ones that had tried to devour Cox earlier. Instead, they were more reminiscent of giant redwoods that he had seen in holovids of Earth.

Had someone planted them here? They seemed curiously out of place.

"Hey," said Babe. "There's something up with these trees."

The kid's gaze darted back and forth. A few seconds later, his eagle eyes stuck on one particular tree. It had a massive trunk - bigger than the grav tank they had just destroyed.

The sniper scrambled over and ran a hand along the mossy bark. Smith crouched as another blast whipped through the forest.

"Why aren't they chasing us?" asked Cox.

Smith twirled a finger in a broad circle.

"They're surrounding us first. Don't worry - they'll be here soon enough. If we don't find that hatch, we're dead meat."

"Got it!" shouted Babe.

Something hissed inside the trunk and a man-sized section of the bark swung outward. Behind it was only darkness. Without waiting, Babe pulled out his pistol and leapt inside. Cox and Stoltz were next. Smith swung a leg inside and paused before fishing out a pair of hover grenades.

He tossed both straight up in the air. Twenty feet up, their ascent abruptly halted. Two tiny beeps informed him that they were now armed. If anyone passed underneath, the munitions would detonate and send several thousand fragments raining down on the pursuer.

***

The door shut behind him with a soft clatter. The interior of the tree was coated in smooth concrete. In the middle of the floor was a hatch, below which a staircase unfolded toward the forest floor. The rest of the team was already descending the narrow steps.

At the base of the stairs was a long hallway. Smith swung open the door at the end of it and walked into a giant concrete tunnel that might have belonged on a highway. It was as wide as four lanes and extended for as far as he could see. The length of it was lit by the harsh glare of white fluorescent lights that were embedded along the walls.

Smith let out a surprise-filled expletive over the comms link.

"Is this the same size as the other tunnel you found?"

"Nope," said Cox. "This one's huge."

"That must have been a branch or something," said Stoltz. "You could fly a lander through here."

Each footfall echoed along the giant tunnel, adding to Smith's growing sense of vulnerability. Scanning the ground, he had expected to see tire marks or footprints. Instead, there was only a clinical sterility to the paved surface.

"I wonder why Andrews didn't tell us about this tunnel," said Smith.

"Maybe he didn't know about it," said Stoltz. "RJ had to pull off some serious moves to access that archive."

"Hey, I got something here," said Babe. The kid had gone on ahead to scout things out.

"A huge set of double doors," he added. "Blast doors. And - oh - looks like I'm on camera here."

Smith couldn't help but wait a beat for White to issue an order. When he remembered that the sergeant was dead, he chided himself then spoke up.

"Hold right there, Babe. We're on the way."

Two minutes later, they reached the scout's position. His back was against the wall and his pistol was aimed straight at the door. Smith slid a hand along its cool shiny surface. Its tangy smell brought him back to a former life on Grimgate, where his parents and older brothers had toiled ceaselessly in the airless mines.

Cox leveled his launcher tube at the door and gestured to Smith.

"Get back."

"We're not blasting our way in," said Smith. "Not with a hundred launchers. Where's the camera, Babe?"

The kid pointed up to the top of the door where three lenses peered back down at the team.

"You think anyone's watching?" asked Stoltz.

"If it's the mercs, they already know we're here," said Smith. "If it's someone beyond that blast door, the same goes."

"If the mercs knew about this tunnel, we would've found them down here by now," said Babe.

"Well, let's take a minute and see if we can catch the attention of whoever's beyond that door. Otherwise, we keep going. Heath and Hayes are still waiting for us."

Smith waved his arms toward the camera and gestured to his helmet. Using his fingers, he counted off the frequency for his comms, one digit at a time. When he was finished, he repeated it once more. As soon as he finished, static crackled over the helmet.

"Are you here to rescue us? Or kill us?" said the voice.

"We're here to find two of our men," said Smith. "By the way, who exactly is 'us'?"

"There's a dozen of us," came the answer. "We work at the outpost. Did work there, anyway. Before they came."

"Twelve?" asked Babe. "That base is big enough for two hundred. Where's the rest of you?"

"Dead. Their ship was shot down as they fled from the planet."

"You have a data card in there?" asked Smith.

After a long pause, the answer came back. "We have extremely sensitive information stored in here."

"We've been sent to retrieve it. We'll take you back with us. Why would you think we're down here to kill you?"

"The information on the card," said the voice, "is highly incriminating in nature."

"Incriminating for who?" asked Smith. This felt like a game and he was quickly tiring of it.

"Key members of our defense forces. Men and women who have compromised our military secrets to an enemy alliance. You're with Andrews, aren't you? He's with them."

Smith flinched as though he'd been slapped. Had Andrews really sent them down here to retrieve a data card full of evidence against him? It didn't make any real sense to send both mercs and a Space Infantry team down to get a data card – unless the mercs couldn't manage to locate it on their own.

"Hold on," said Stoltz. "Why would Andrews send us down here to search for it? Seems a whole lot easier to just nuke the place and be done with it."

The voice behind the door spoke in matter-of-fact tones, as if it were utterly bored with the conversation already.

"Nuclear authorization would only be given as a last resort. The loss of a Space Infantry team would be enough for that."

"Come on guys," said Stoltz. "That doesn't make a bit of sense. We're on the same side here."

Smith's mind reeled. What if the mercs had been set up too? Andrews could have told them to expect a Space Infantry team to land on the planet and ambush them at the outpost. It was clear enough that the squad had been compromised from the get-go.

He could see the plan working on two levels: hire an army of mercenaries to find a data card and kill off a Space Infantry team. If they accomplished the former, the evidence against Andrews would be secured. If not, the loss of an SI team would be enough to justify the destruction of the planet – and the evidence with it.

And just like that, General Andrews would have everything wrapped up in a neat little bow.

Smith felt like he was on the verge of falling down a very deep hole. Right at the edge of insanity and reason, he perched there - unwilling to accept the conclusions. And yet - everything fit.

If the data card existed, and the disembodied voice he was talking with was speaking the truth, they were all in far more danger than they had even considered. Had the Union gone mad? Andrews had a clean record, but he was one of the most outspoken men in the union for going to war against the growing menace that had slowly surrounded the borders of Earth's outer colonies.

"Your transmissions…uh…encrypted?" asked Smith. At last he understood the reason for the suspicious greeting.

"Yes. We're following your frequency hops right now with a device of our own."

"What kind of proof do you have?"

"Burst transmissions from Andrews to several leaders of the military. One of our analysts stumbled on them a few months ago. The messages were coded but we broke them. It's…kind of what we do down here. Two days ago, one of our men disappeared along with a shuttle craft. I can only guess he went off to warn Andrews about what we'd found."

It all sounded plausible but Smith knew very little of decryption. Either way, there was no time to pick it apart. With forty minutes left before *The Luzon* arrived, there was maybe just enough time to rescue Hayes and Heath then return here and get the rest of these men aboard.

For now, he would take it on faith that rescuing the station staff and retrieving the data card were mission critical. Whether or not the Space Infantry was being used as a political pawn was something for someone at a higher pay grade to fret over.

"Here's the deal," said Smith. "I couldn't care less about Andrews and the data card. We need to get moving. Once we rescue our men, we'll be back here to get you. You'll have a tight window to get out of here before the whole planet gets blown apart."

"How do we know if we can trust you? You might shoot us all and steal the data card. You might be one of them!"

"I'm not going to spend time trying to convince you," said Smith. "Either you come with us or you stay down here and die anyway. Suit yourselves."

FINAL COUNTDOWN

When they arrived at the end of the tunnel, Smith watched the icons pop up on his helmet display. Two baby blue diamond shapes marked the location of Hayes and Heath. It was like Christmas morning and a birthday all rolled into one. They were alive - at least for now - and even better, they were close by.

The hatch for this particular tunnel opened right up in the middle of the control room. If they could act quickly, they would only need to climb up then make a dash down a long corridor before reaching the storage room where they were being held.

"You see it?" asked Smith. The others nodded.

"If Andrews is in on this, he's told them already," said Cox. "They know we're coming. It's a trap."

"Maybe," said Smith. "You want out?"

"Hell no."

Smith came up out of the hatch with his weapon drawn. He shot the first man he saw. The laser blast cleaved into the merc's chest, leaving a smoking hole to mark its impact.

A pair of shots swept by Smith's head before he rolled out and scrambled toward the cover of a nearby desk. Stoltz popped up like a gopher out of a hole and nailed two mercs in the head. Three enemies down. So many more to go.

Smith kicked the door leading to the corridor. It was empty. He sensed the trap that lay in the rooms on either side. They would get halfway down the hallway only to find the enemies popping out of each room and laying down a huge volume of fire at close range.

He nodded over to Cox and Stoltz. "Grenades."

The motion sensing explosives were tossed toward the doors on either side of the corridor. When all six were gone, Smith sprinted along its length as he waited for the inevitable. Sure enough, halfway toward the storage room, the doors swung open and the grenades went off.

BOOMBOOMBOOM!

Rifle fire swept back and forth along the length of the hallway. Babe tossed a grenade into one of the rooms as he ran and ducked. The doorway erupted in a geyser of smoke and fire. A pair of corpses littered the ground.

Smith watched in horror as a giant covered with body armor stepped out of the nearest door with a multi-barrel in his hand. The huge apparatus whirred and rotated as it spat out a hundred rounds.

Shots ripped through the hallway, punching holes the size of basketballs into doors and walls. Babe charged and leapt up at the man, who knocked him out of the air with a huge fist that sent him sprawling backward. The kid yelped in pain.

Smith fired two shots dead center into the mercenary's bulky armored chest. Neither of them got through but it was enough to halt the onslaught of fire. The multi-barrel spooled up and Cox let loose a feral scream. Something buzzed by Smith's helmet and the next thing he knew, the world burst apart in a harsh glow.

The helmet dampeners kicked in but just barely enough to avoid becoming deaf and blind. Staggering around with his hands on his head, he tried to piece together bits of thought into some kind of coherence. Stoltz was in front of him, firing off a short burst at something that Smith couldn't see. Babe rushed up and shoved him hard to the ground.

"Stay down!" he shouted.

Smith spotted Cox grappling with the behemoth, who lay on the ground like a turtle on its back. Meanwhile, Stoltz and Babe were trading fire with someone shooting from inside the storage room.

Smith got up and staggered toward the door. As he reached Cox, the big man smashed a fist down on the merc's helmet. The brain-jarring punches continued until Smith pulled a vibroblade out and handed it to his fellow teammate. Cox seized it and plunged the knife down again and again into the enemy mercenary's heaving chest.

With the grisly work done, Smith plucked a flashbang from his bag and tossed it into the storage room. The concussion was tremendous - enough to send tremors along the smashed walls and doorways. Babe and Stoltz rushed in with Smith close behind.

When he arrived in the room, he found Heath on the floor, his hands bound together with paracord. Hayes staggered around the center of the room in a daze. In her hand, she clutched a pistol pointed at the ground. Heath was the first to speak through a haze of painful grunts.

"Take her out guys," said Heath. "She's with them."

Smith's gut roiled with anger and confusion. Was Heath for real? He would take no chances.

"Hayes. Drop it," said Smith. "You have three guns trained on you right now. Lift that pistol up and you're dead."

She plopped on the floor and took off the helmet to reveal a face full of resignation. Her lips were drawn tight and her eyes scrunched together as if in anguish. Lisa Hayes looked like hell. Smith eyed at the pistol in her hands and took a cautious step toward her.

"It's true," she said. "He's right."

Stoltz nodded at her with a sneer. "Why? At least tell us that much."

"I was just so tired of fixing up other people's mistakes. This little secret war we've been fighting - it's time to let someone else do the dying. The whole Union is just kept together like a patchwork, and we're the little plumbers who get sent out every day to repair it.

"We're out there fighting and dying and for what? No one will ever know what we did. Hell, no one will even know our real names."

Smith focused on her pistol. Each tiny twitch of her finger plucked at his nerves. Enough suffering had already happened here. Smith wanted to walk out of this place with her, if she would let him.

"You want to spread the dying around, Hayes? Is that it?" Stoltz's voice was full of contempt for her. It was hard not to listen to her and wonder how long she had hidden these feelings.

Only this morning, she had come into the squad bay for something. She was trying to talk to him. Or more importantly, to be listened to. Smith had belittled her instead. There was another chance to talk near the airlock – but Smith had been so wrapped up in his own pain that he hadn't bothered to consider that she was even worse-off.

Hayes rolled her eyes. "You think I want war? Look at what we've been busy doing the past few years. The war's already here. And if we don't fight them here and now with everything we've got, they'll be here at our doorstep soon enough. What else is left?

"They'll keep sending us out as fodder again and again until we're dead or useless. Andrews was right - we start and finish this thing on our own terms and build a better future for humanity. I know you don't like it - you don't have to. The truth is the beginning of wars don't really matter. Only the ends. Join me on this one. Andrews needs you too."

Smith stood up on unsteady feet as Heath chuckled.

"Bravo," he hissed. "You practice that in front of a mirror?"

"What was the plan?" asked Smith. "At least tell me that much."

Hayes scowled at the ground as she spoke.

"We were supposed to work together with the mercs to find that data card," she said. "But then the shooting started and no one would back down. They just got angrier as you killed more and more of them. I tried to talk to them. Tried to convince them to cease fire. I was trying to stop the bleeding. No one would listen."

"Traitor," spat Heath.

Hayes shot a glare over at him.

"I should have known you'd never understand. Never listen. You'll ship me off to some prison colony now and laugh while I'm rotting in a cell. That's never gonna happen."

As she raised the pistol to her temple, Smith leapt at her. The struggle that ensued was short and one-sided. He slashed at her with the flat of his arm. The weapon tumbled out of her grip and spun through the air.

Hayes tried to squirm out of Smith's grip as he wrapped his other arm around her and pinned his teammate to the ground. She cursed and flailed as Babe pounced and snatched the gun off the ground. The angry whimpers that filled the room subsided moments later, and he left her there in a heap.

"How much time we got?" he asked Stoltz.

"Ten minutes."

"Get Heath untied, then let's go. Hayes - I'm giving you two options and you'd better hurry up and take one of them. Option A - you come with us and we figure things out aboard the dropship. Try to sabotage our escape and we'll make you wish you took your own life. Option B - you stay here and get nuked by The Luzon. What's it gonna be?"

The note of fury disappeared and Hayes' face transformed into steel resolution. It was the same one he'd seen when they were nearing the end of the four hundred push-up punishment that White had assigned them.

"I want to help. Let's get out of here."

Heath rubbed his freed wrists and squinted his eyes in her direction. "I'm watching you, Hayes."

Smith keyed his comms transmitter to the lander's frequency. Rob answered.

"*The Luzon's* already here," he said. "You'd better get your butts out of that facility. Let me know where to pick you up."

"Nothing fancy," said Smith. "I'm sending you the coordinates now."

They bolted back toward the command center and slipped down the hatch that led to the massive tunnel.

Along its length, were heaps of bodies sprawled along the pavement. Dead mercenaries were everywhere. A glimpse above them revealed a shot-out turret in the wall. It dangled limply from the wires and cables. Beneath it was a mound of brass casings.

The blast door was now open with the console beside it rewired and hacked. Beyond it were more bodies - it was obvious the outpost staff had fought to the last man. All of them had died during the assault.

"Four minutes 'til we're done," said Smith. "Thirty-five seconds to search for the data card and we're out."

The team scrambled through the room. After digging through pockets of corpses and rifling through cabinets and drawers, time was up and nobody had found anything that even resembled what they were seeking.

"That's it," said Smith. "We're out."

The team hastened along the corridor. Smith wondered how many enemies would be there to greet them when they emerged from the hatch, then decided it didn't really matter. His fate was entirely out of his control now.

Rob would either be there with the lander or he wouldn't. If so, they were saved. If not, they would be greeted with a hail of gunfire just before the nuke went off and burned everyone to a crisp. The only thing left was to hope - and keep running.

Smith was first out of the hatch. The wooded area immediately around them was flattened, thanks largely due to the explosives he had planted before descending into the tunnel. He was pleased to see that his hasty booby-traps had managed to decapitate several mercenaries.

Above them, the lander loomed, its engines straining to maintain a careful hover as laser blasts from the ground sparked off the fuselage. RJ squatted in the bubble canopy slung underneath the vehicle and sprayed a long stream of autocannon fire at the ship's attackers.

"You better hustle" said Rob.

Six lines dropped from the undercarriage and each member of the infantry grabbed on - all except Hayes. As the lines reeled up toward the open belly of the lander, Smith waved at her.

"Come on. You're still one of us."

Hayes didn't budge. Instead, she snapped off a salute and stood there as the lander's bay door sealed. Smith stared at her through the window as the lander pivoted. As they shot up into orbit, he lamented his own failure.

Was there something he could have done to prevent all this? Everyone grappled with these feelings. Why had they never discussed it? He had always assumed there would be time for it someday.

Now it was too late and "someday" would never come.

They were in low orbit when the first bomb struck. The lander bucked like a wild animal as Rob angled the nose straight up to get away from the blast. Each team member tumbled amid the turbulence and landed back down hard on the deck of the cabin. The torrent of bumps and jolts gradually lessened over the next thirty seconds.

"Look!" Babe shouted. The kid was seated near the back of the lander, facing the rear ports that offered a view of the planet below.

Smith forced himself to turn his head. The planet's usual layer of cloud cover had been ripped away by the sheer destructive power of a hundred 100-megaton bombs. Across the planet's surface, a series of widening circles of flame and dust grew outward.

Massive shockwaves rippled along the landscape. The island turned black and featureless. Little green dots of forests were wiped out and the seething ocean soon became enraged.

What must have been five-hundred-foot waves thundered over the coastline and swept over the hills. Just like that, the island was gone - replaced by a dirty irradiated flood. Somewhere down there in that swamp were the ashes of a woman Smith had once held in his arms.

The lander shot past the giant deadly form of *The Luzon*. Fresh from discharging its deadly arsenal of nuclear weapons on the planet below, perched there like a dark angry god. Smith wondered if it would turn its batteries on *The Mule* as it glided past.

If Andrews suspected they knew something, there was more than enough motive and means to blast the team out of the sky and call it a day. No loose ends.

It's exactly the way Smith would have played it.

A pair of long rectangular cannons on *The Luzon's* midships rotated slowly toward them, as if noticing the lander's presence for the first time. They were the size of skyscrapers and had the power to wipe out any enemy. Flying this close to the ship seemed like an act of audacity.

"You see those guns pointed right at us?" asked Cox.

Rob's voice crackled over the headset. "Yeah, I see that. We're just gonna keep going. Whistle past the graveyard."

Smith couldn't have agreed more. There was nothing else to do. For the hundredth time today, his life was in the hands of someone else's better judgment. He heard Rob talking over the radio to hail *The Luzon*.

No response.

The cannons tracked the lander's path as Rob banked the ship and gently rolled it to a new heading. Smith didn't realize he was sweating until the beads slid down off his forehead and dripped on the deck.

MARS UNLEASHED

No shots came. *The Mule* made its way back to the dropship and docked in its belly. When the hangar bay doors boomed shut, everyone let out a collective sigh of relief all at once.

Smith chuckled at how they had once again ridden the razor-thin edge of peril to the very end.

Still, death had claimed its due.

The team was down by two members. Neither White nor Hayes would be replaced quickly or easily. Smith oversaw the team now and he would have to learn how to run missions on a shoestring economy of manpower.

White had been a mentor of sorts, but the man had worked like a lion behind the scenes to keep everything running as smooth as possible despite the incredible demands that had been placed on them.

Smith would have to step into his shoes and learn to do the same as he went along. It had been one hell of a battlefield promotion and Smith wasn't sure he craved the added responsibility pressing down on his shoulders. After all, he had been ready to run off on everyone less than twenty-four hours ago.

The good news was that Davis was out of critical care and beginning to walk again. Countless advances in medicine over the past centuries had made a good number of permanent and life-altering injuries into temporary and recoverable variety.

Despite all that, it seemed that the body's hardware still needed a minimum amount of time to properly heal. It had been that way for hundreds of years. Scientific progress was no longer measured in leaps and bounds by cloistered geniuses in lab coats.

Everything had become so complex that advances came in drips and drabs and were only arrived at thanks to the efforts of thousands - sometimes millions - of scientists working in highly organized teams with disparate backgrounds.

Before the weapons were even stowed in the armory, Gideon informed the crew that General Andrews wanted to meet with them immediately. Smith wondered what to say.

The Luzon was still in orbit and though *Thor's Hammer* was much sturdier than the lander, it stood no chance at all in a battle with a cruiser. He could certainly reveal what he learned from Hayes and the anonymous analyst he had spoken with on the planet, but without any solid proof such claims would venture into insubordination territory. Without the data card, there was no conspiracy - only guesses.

"We'll be there in a few minutes," he told the artificial intelligence.

Cox folded his arms. "I would rather stuff a load of gunpowder up my keester and sit on a bonfire than deal with that guy right now."

"Now that I'd like to see," said Heath.

Smith paused as he watched the men turn to leave. Something was still pulling at the back of his mind.

"Heath - wait up," he said.

The tall lanky private turned, his face covered in bruises and several cuts from his ordeal back at the outpost.

"What happened down there between you and Hayes?" said Smith. "They torture you or what?"

"Why would they do that? There wasn't anything I knew that Hayes didn't know already."

"How come they kept you alive then?"

Heath shrugged. "They wanted to kill me, but Hayes stepped in. Said I was insurance. She knew Andrews was gonna nuke the planet if they couldn't find the card. She said I'd be enough of an incentive to stop it from happening. No one would dare nuke an SI team."

"They believed her?"

"What choice did they have?" He turned and strolled away.

Smith stood there for a minute, wondering if he could trust the answer. One of the team had slipped up and been turned by a conniving group of men intent on bringing war and death to humanity. Were there more?

There was no way of knowing until someone showed their hand. One thing was clear - it would take a long time for the psychological wounds to heal. Hayes' failure was not just her own - it was never that simple. If Andrews had approached him in a moment of weakness, he might just as well have joined her.

Minutes later, he sat in the briefing room and waited for the general's holographic image to appear.

"What's the plan here?" asked Stoltz.

"Just the facts," said Smith.

If Andrews really did harbor some secret desire to foment a war between the Union and alien alliances, he showed no hint of it in his words or expressions during the debrief.

Smith kept things as straight and to the point, mentioning nothing of Hayes or the real contents of the data card. The mission, as prescribed by its parameters, was a failure. Nothing of real value had been achieved on the planet.

"Not quite true," said Andrews. "When we put these events together with the raids on the other systems, we have a more thorough picture of what's been happening here. We've captured several mercenaries in our other operations and they have all confessed to being hired by hostile governments.

"What we have just been party to is an opening salvo in a seething conflict between humanity and its foes. I intend to go directly to the presidency and announce these findings. Although it hasn't been declared yet, we are unofficially at war as of this moment.

"I want you to be prepared for the coming conflict, so stick to your training schedule and be ready at a moment's notice. We'll all be very busy in the coming days and weeks."

Smith listened to the hollow words and tried to keep his face poker straight. Stoltz started to say something and received a hard kick under the table for his efforts.

When the briefing ended, the ship's ionic drive spun up and *Thor's Hammer* departed the system for Station Hale. As the craft traveled through the folds of space, Smith gazed out the windows and tried to picture what the future would bring for him and the team.

There would be more death and killing, but there would also be family.

He would stay with them until the end.

THE MULE

THOR'S HAMMER

OUTPOST 13

STATION HALE

OUTPOST MAP

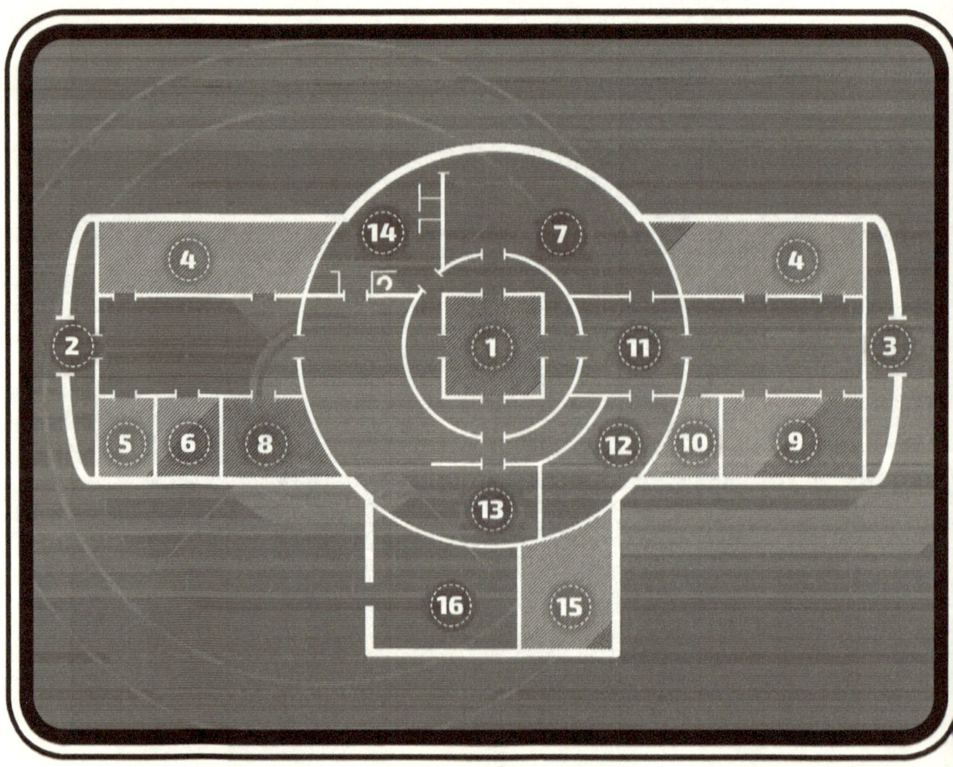

1. **Command Center**
2. **Security Office**
3. **Security Office**
4. **Quarters**
5. **Supply**
6. **Storage**
7. **Intel**
8. **Exercise**
9. **Cafeteria**
10. **Commons**
11. **Briefing Room**
12. **Labs**
13. **Analysis**
14. **Private Offices**
15. **Tunnel Access Hatch**
16. **Comms**
17. **Vehicle Storage/ Maintenance**

TACTICAL BREAKDOWN

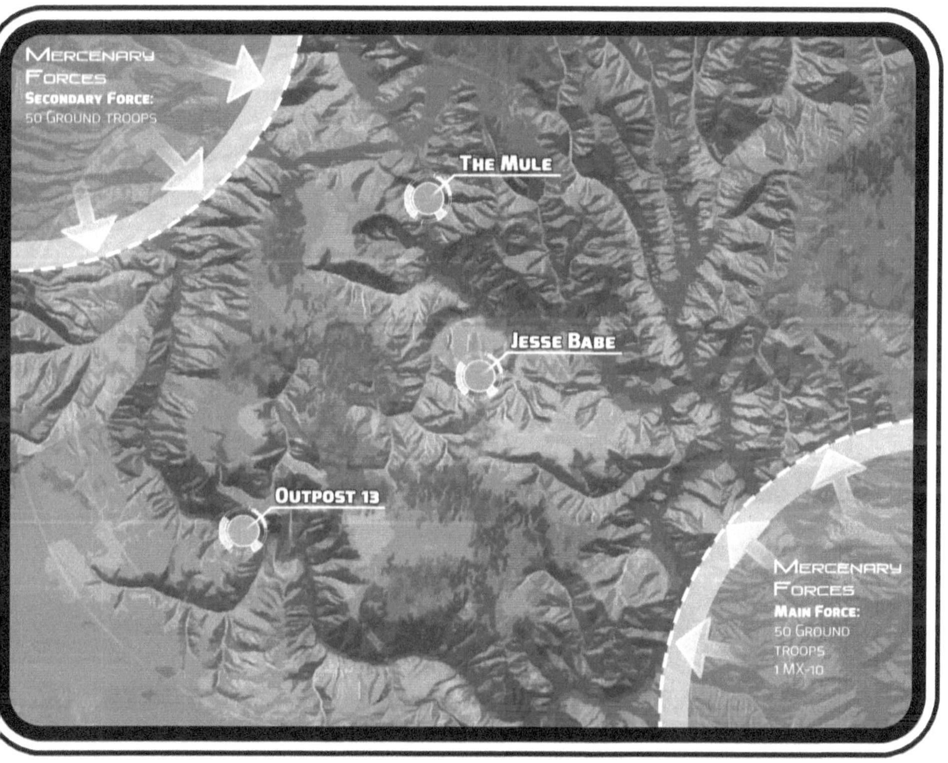

MX-10 GRAV TANK

ABOUT THE AUTHORS
- Brad Smith and David Heath -

Brad Smith is a freelance writer and game designer who lives in Japan. He has a keen interest in the topic of the late Cold War, which has fed his creative output. He has authored eight books set in an alternate World War III: 1985 universe. His blog can be found at: www.hexsides.com. You can also access his books on the Amazon.com store page. Several of his stories are available through Lock 'n Load Publishing.

His main interests are writing, wargaming, and spending time with his family. He recently designed "NATO Air Commander" and the soon to be released "That Others May Live" both published by Hollandspiele. Two of his favorite wargames are "Gulf Strike" and "The Korean War" from Victory Games.

David Heath has been playing games in some way or another for most of my life. They are and have always been a large part of who I am. I knew since high school, I wanted to write, design, and develop great games and stories. I owe a great deal of gratitude to Mark Herman and Eric Lee Smith for giving me the opportunity as an intern at Victory Games. It started a fire that has never gone out in me.

I am currently the owner and operator of Lock 'n Load Publishing as well as being the founder and President of The Gamers Network, Matrix Games, Tri-Games, Strategic Games Publications, and at one point, the owner of The Wargamer. I have owned a few other businesses over the years, but I always keep coming back to gaming.

My other interests include music, movies, and technology, and how I can combine my interests together. I give praise and thanks to God for blessing me and allowing me to follow my dreams.

ABOUT THE EDITOR
- Hans Korting -

I have been reading books about (military) aviation history all of my life, and this way the connection with military history is easily made. Main interest is WWII, but I also enjoy reading up on and playing games about WWI, modern-era warfare, the American Civil War, Napoleonics, and more. First game ever was bought in an American book store in Amsterdam, Avalon Hill's D-Day '77. Next game was SPI's Arnhem, and a whole range of games has followed since. Putting my hands, or rather eyes, where my mouth is, I next decided to help out proofreading rulebooks. Some gaming magazines were next, like War Diary magazine. I also write about boardwargames for Ducosim's (DutchConflictSimulation) Spel! magazine, and sometimes try to write a decent article for a magazine too. Daytime job is at a small insurance broker as a claims handler.

AUDIO BOOK EDITION
- Narrated By: Othello Lofton -

Othello Lofton was an audiobook narrator before audiobooks were a thing. As a child he spent many a weekend afternoon in the library or cruising the flea market for used paperbacks of the SF persuasion. He would then spend the rest of the week, reading his treasures out loud, voicing the characters and reenacting their adventures. Nowadays, you'll find this self-professed comic book nerd in his home studio, The Danger Room, reliving those childhood stories in front of a microphone. And he's glad you decided to come along on the adventure.

WHAT IS THE SPACE INFANTRY GAME SERIES
- by Blackwell Hird -

I am the Co-Designer and Lead Graphic Designer for the Space Infantry Resurgence series. At Lock 'n Load Publishing we publish tabletop, computer games, and book series with a strategy theme. These stories are inspired by the kind of stories shared by friends as we discuss our gaming adventures.

This book was develop to expand our adventures in the Space Infantry Resurgence universe. Thanks to many, including David Heath and Brad Smith, for their vision and passion for wanting to expand this series.

This story use a number of things from our Space Infantry game series, specifically the lore and terminology and even the occasional moments inspired by game events. This added a new level to our stories and added the ability and similarity for these men and women to live on in each of our games.

Some of you may be wondering what the Space Infantry game series is all about. The Space Infantry (SI) series is a dynamic squad level rogue-like exploration and combat board game series centered on building a squad to tackle randomly generated missions against ever evolving enemies from 17 different races, all within a fictional science fiction setting. With unparalleled artwork and a focus on solo play and random chance to keep the player always on their toes, each action-packed engagement plays out cinematically.

Decisions have lasting consequences, both on mission and in future missions. Tactical leadership is key. Unique abilities and synergies enhance effectiveness. And detailed objectives based on the scenario layout encourages bold gameplay. There is even a Multi-player module for those mission where you need an extra set of hands.

Random missions and squad building are the heart of Space Infantry, but we have a fully fleshed out campaign system for you to take your squad through multiple mission in a row, and really test your decision making skills. There are also options to play fully narrative campaigns with sequential missions, head to head against an overlord played by your friend, you can play against a horde of enemies to see how long you survive, and even alter the biomes and difficulty of the missions you play on the fly. Your choice of squad members and gear is just as diverse as well, from civilian specialists, to snipers, heavy weapons, flame throwers, Zero-G teams and armored Vehicles. We also have free downloadable game walkthroughs, making the game series more accessible than ever to new players.

Whether you are a fan of science fiction or a good solo experience, the Space Infantry series has you covered with an absolutely packed box and expansion, including an evolving storyline to follow as you play through ear game in the series. With Space Infantry the gaming never ends. It's Squad-level tactical combat and exploration at its best!

Another Day in tyhe Corps

The United Systems are under Siege. What started as isolated incursions in the Deep range, Inner Reach and even the Jovian Habitats, has escalated into all out war against our species. Enemies too numerous to count are pushing us on all fronts and we've been losing ground with every passing year. Worse still, a new Xenos Mind has emerged; some dark hand guiding the alien threats against us in new and unpredictable ways.

To answer this threat and regain the offensive, a new Space Infantry Core has been formed. Armed with cutting edge weaponry, vehicles, and strategic options, we now have the means to drive back the Xeno threat, from the depths of their hives to the cold of space.

Space Infantry: Resurgence is a solo to 2 player game in which players will build a Space Infantry Squad, outfit them with deadly weapons and vehicles, then guide that squad through a multi-mission persistent campaign. Fight alone, as a team, or against another player taking the role of the Xeno Mind.

WORLD AT WAR 85 NOVELS

The Third World War has Begun

Storming the Gap: First Strike reveals the explosive origins of the Third World War and delves into the opening salvos of the conflict between NATO and the Warsaw Pact in a world where the Cold War turns hot in 1985. This epic story is told from a range of viewpoints - through the eyes of the decision-makers in Washington as well as the tankers and infantry fighting through hills and towns of southern Germany.

Based partly on the scenarios from the smash-hit game by Lock 'n Load Publishing World At War 85, each tale is a pulse-pounding narrative of intense Armor clashes that will help determine the fate of the most valuable piece of real estate this side of the Inner German border — the Fulda Gap

As the first volume of a series that tells one version of the war's progress, First Strike can be enjoyed as a companion to the platoon-scale wargame or by casual readers as a close-up view of mechanized combat in a war that never was.

THE SECOND WAVE HAS BEEN UNLEASHED

The forces of the Warsaw Pact storm west over the Inner German Border and unleash devastation on the first days of the conflict. Among the NATO defenders of West Germany are Captain Kurt Mohr and his company of Leopard tanks. Outgunned and outnumbered, the men must conduct vital delaying operations until reinforcements can mobilize to stop the communists in their tracks.

To make matters worse, Mohr's leadership is challenged at every step by internal politics that jeopardize the mission and his men's lives. Each critical decision brings the company to the brink of tearing itself apart - posing a threat as dangerous as the enemy itself. Can Mohr keep his men together and stay alive or will his first day of war be his last?

WORLD AT WAR 85 NOVELS

SOMETHING THE SOVIETS DIDN'T PLAN ON

It is May 1985 and World War III rages in Central Europe. Fledgling insurgent groups in the East Bloc fight for independence from their Soviet overlords. America pledges to help. Among the teams of US military advisers are two Vietnam War veterans, sent in to assist an East German major named Werner Brandt and his motley band of fighters. Their objectives are to help destroy Soviet military reinforcements as they speed towards the frontlines and to eliminate the Russian garrison in control of Saxony. It won't be easy – Brandt is consumed with a lust for vengeance that threatens to derail his own operations.

Captain Joe Ricci and Sergeant Ned Littlejohn are about to enter a combat zone for the first time in nearly fifteen years. With them, they bring the scarred memories of their Vietnam experiences. As the stakes climb higher and the battle to survive grows more intense, each decision could lead to the liberation of a nation or their own downfall.

THE SOVIET INVASION CONTINUES

First Lieutenant Darren White is trapped behind enemy lines with the remnants of his cavalry troop. Together with his second-in-command, Maurice Fitzgerald, he waits for the right opportunity to strike back at the Russians in occupied West Germany.

As they conduct joint operations with a Special Forces team in the Fulda Gap, a terrible secret is uncovered. The Soviets have found a sure-fire way to win the war. It's up to White and Fitzgerald to stop them. A daring operation might just be enough to make or break the Soviet war effort in Fulda. Will Fitzgerald and White's personal differences doom the attempt?

HEROES AGAINST THE RED STAR

The Red Star Strikes!

It's the spring of 1985 and the Cold War has turned Hot. Out of the dawn sky, Soviet paratroopers are being whisked across the West German border. On the ground, the 1st Tank Division and 33rd Motor Rifle Regiment are rolling toward key command-and-control targets. NATO has to mobilize quickly. World War III has begun, and once again Western Europe is the focal point.

In Heroes Against the Red Star, the Lock 'n Load Tactical Series presents the sweeping rush of the Soviet Red Army, from the shock of the ambitious opening offensive on May 14th against American-held positions in West Germany to the furious rush to Paris, in June, against emboldened French forces

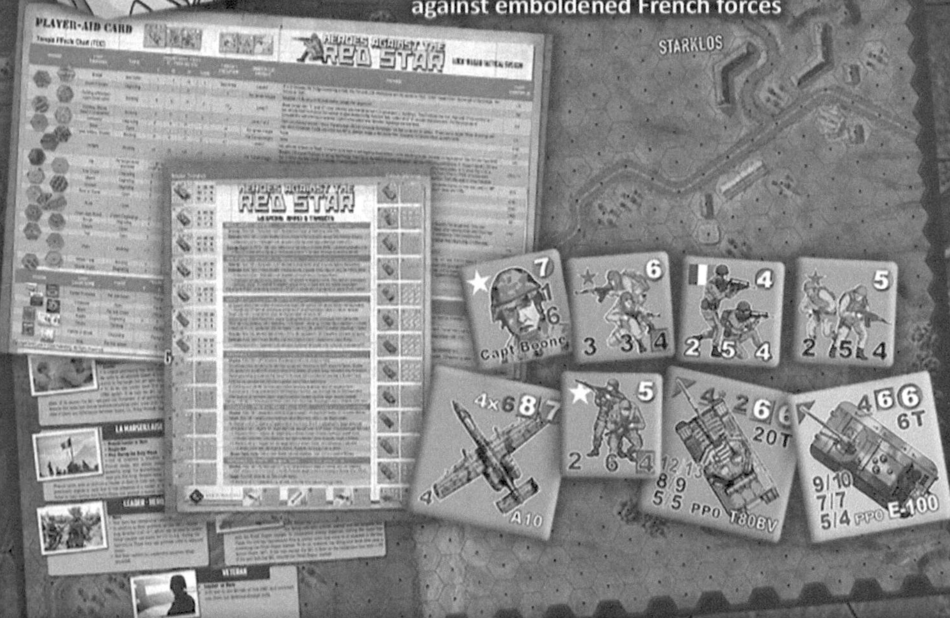

www.ingramcontent.com/pod-product-compliance
Lightning Source LLC
Chambersburg PA
CBHW021203110726
47900CB00002B/715